Early
SCIENCE
Encyclopedias

SPACE

by Meg Marquardt

Early Encyclopedias

An Imprint of Abdo Reference
abdobooks.com

abdobooks.com

Published by Abdo Reference, a division of ABDO, PO Box 398166, Minneapolis, Minnesota 55439.

Printed in China.
052024
092024

THIS BOOK CONTAINS RECYCLED MATERIALS

Editor: Marie Pearson
Series Designers: Candice Keimig, Joshua Olson
Production Designer: Ryan Gale

Library of Congress Control Number: 2023949607

Publisher's Cataloging-in-Publication Data

Names: Marquardt, Meg, author.
Title: Space / by Meg Marquardt
Description: Minneapolis, Minnesota: Abdo Reference, 2025 | Series: Early science encyclopedias | Includes online resources and index.
Identifiers: ISBN 9781098294281 (lib. bdg.) | ISBN 9798384913559 (ebook)
Subjects: LCSH: Space--Juvenile literature. | Space sciences--Juvenile literature. | Outer space--Juvenile literature. | Astronomy--Juvenile literature. | Science--Juvenile literature. | Encyclopedias and dictionaries--Juvenile literature.
Classification: DDC 520--dc23

CONTENTS

What Is Space?

Space is the area beyond Earth's atmosphere. Stars, planets, and galaxies are found in space. At night, humans can see some of those objects more clearly. Scientists who study space are called astronomers.

Almost Empty

Most of space is a vacuum. That means it does not have air. It is almost empty. But some dust and gas float through space.

Scientists do not know exactly how big space is.

Stars are among the space objects people can see from Earth.

The Sun is in a galaxy called the Milky Way.

A Burning Ball

The Sun is a star. A star is a hot ball of burning gas and plasma. The gases in the Sun are hydrogen and helium. When gas gets very hot, it turns into plasma. The Sun's surface is 10,000 degrees Fahrenheit (5,500°C).

Extreme Heat

The Sun's center is about 27 million degrees Fahrenheit (15 million°C). Because the Sun is so hot, it gives off a lot of energy. It makes more energy in less than one second than all humans use in a year.

Sun Layers

The Sun is made of several layers. The core is the center. The photosphere is the layer that people can see.

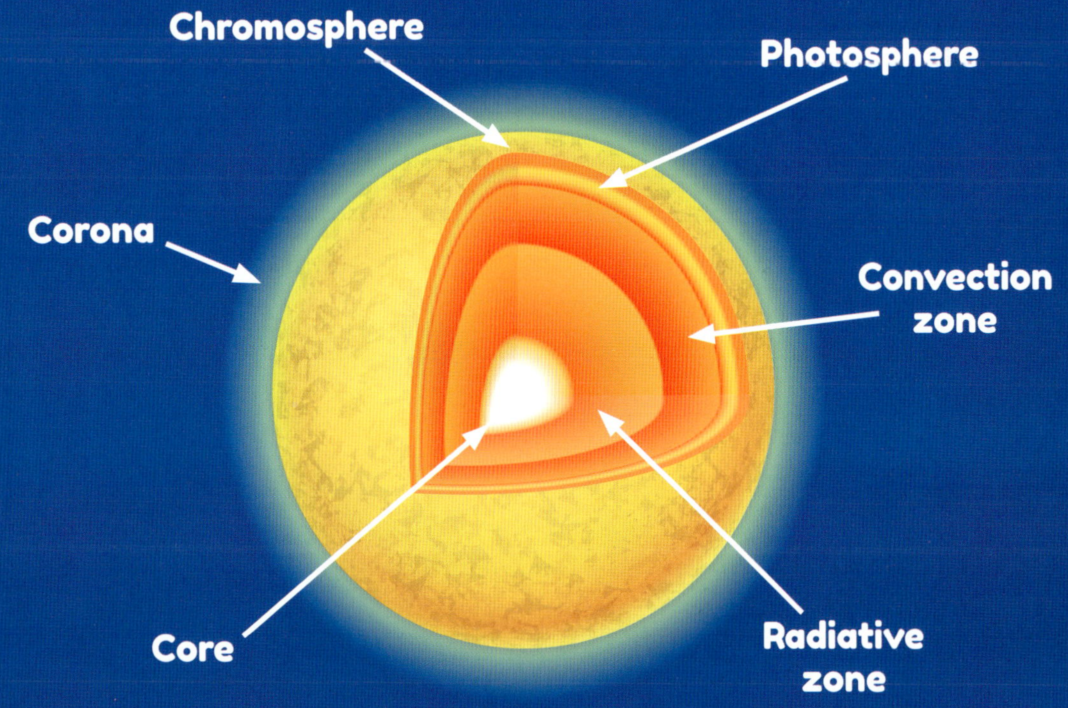

Circling the Sun

The Sun is very large. This means it has strong gravity. The Sun's gravity holds the planets and other objects in orbit. An orbit is a circular path. So these objects orbit the Sun. Together, they make the solar system.

The Solar System

Eight planets orbit the Sun. The white, circular lines show each planet's orbit.

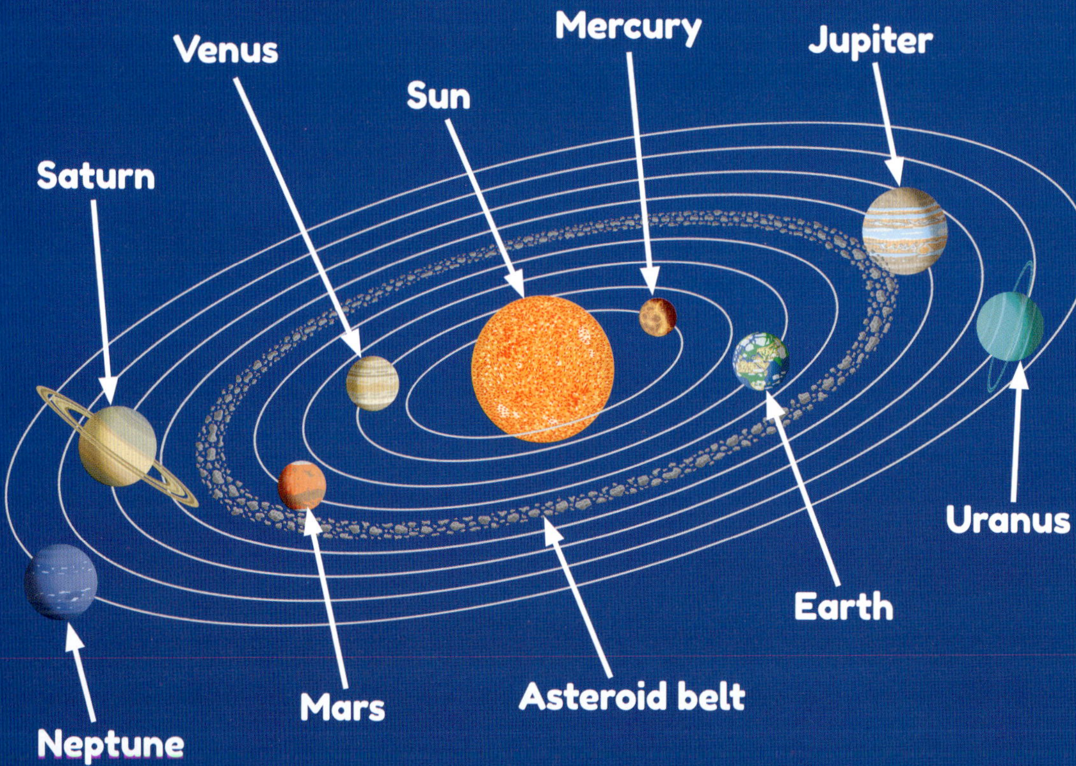

Earth orbits the Sun. The Sun's energy is important for life on Earth.

Sol

Another name for the Sun is Sol. This is why the Sun and the objects that orbit it are called the solar system. Other stars with orbiting objects are called star systems.

Sunspots can be the width of many Earths together.

Sunspots

More than 1 million Earths could fit inside the Sun. The Sun is mostly orange and yellow. It sometimes has dark patches called sunspots. These are cooler parts of the surface.

Bigger Stars

The Sun is an average-sized star. Some stars are much bigger. UY Scuti is 1,700 times larger than the Sun.

Solar Flares

Sometimes an explosion of energy happens on the Sun's surface. This is called a solar flare. Solar flares send energy into space that can sometimes damage electronics on Earth. They often come with a release of plasma that looks like a huge liquid rope.

A solar flare is a bright flash. A coronal mass ejection, *below flash*, is a rope of plasma.

Exploring the Sun

The National Aeronautics and Space Administration (NASA) builds satellites and probes. It uses these machines to explore space. NASA has many satellites that study the Sun.

Some telescopes have filters that let people safely view the Sun from Earth.

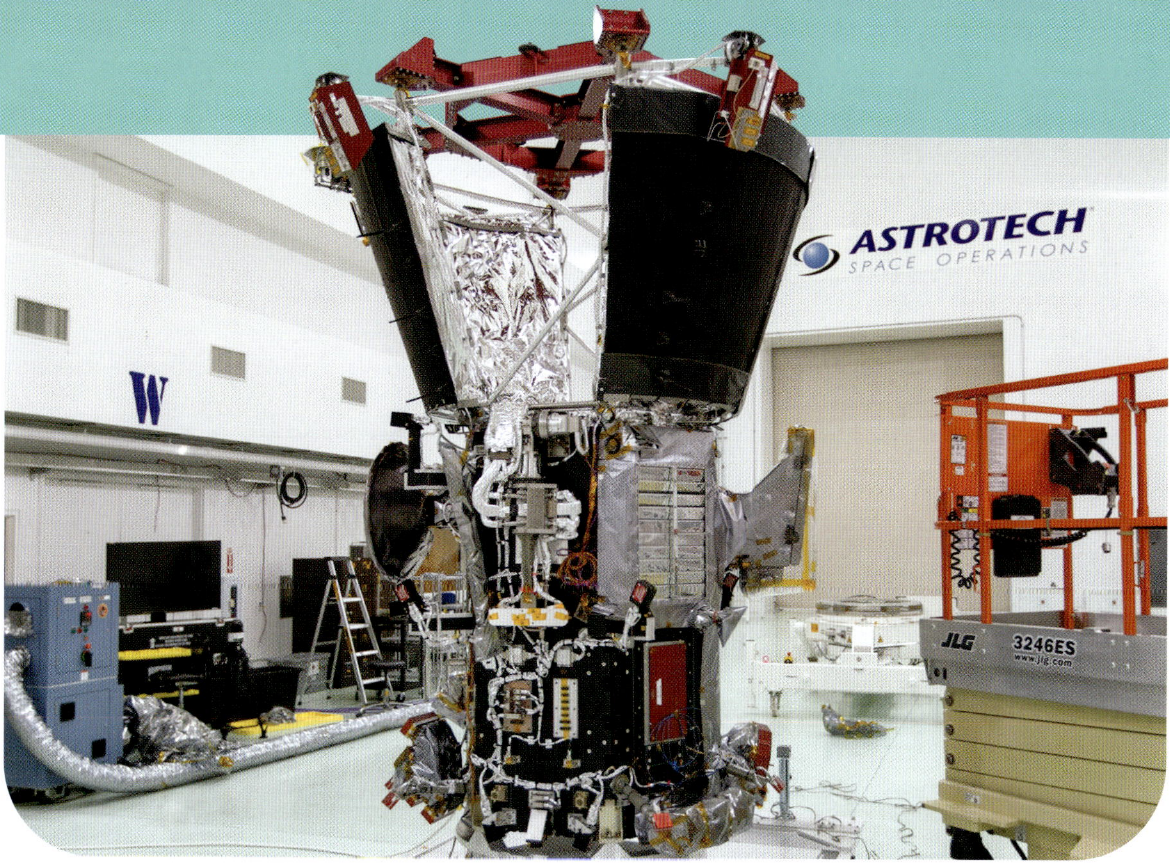

A shield around the top of the *Parker Solar Probe* protects it from the Sun.

Parker Solar Probe

Because the Sun is so hot, it is hard to explore up close. The *Parker Solar Probe* was designed to survive the heat. In 2021, it became the first probe to reach the Sun's atmosphere. Its mission was to get as close to the Sun's surface as possible. It was scheduled to get 4 million miles (6.4 million km) from the surface in 2025.

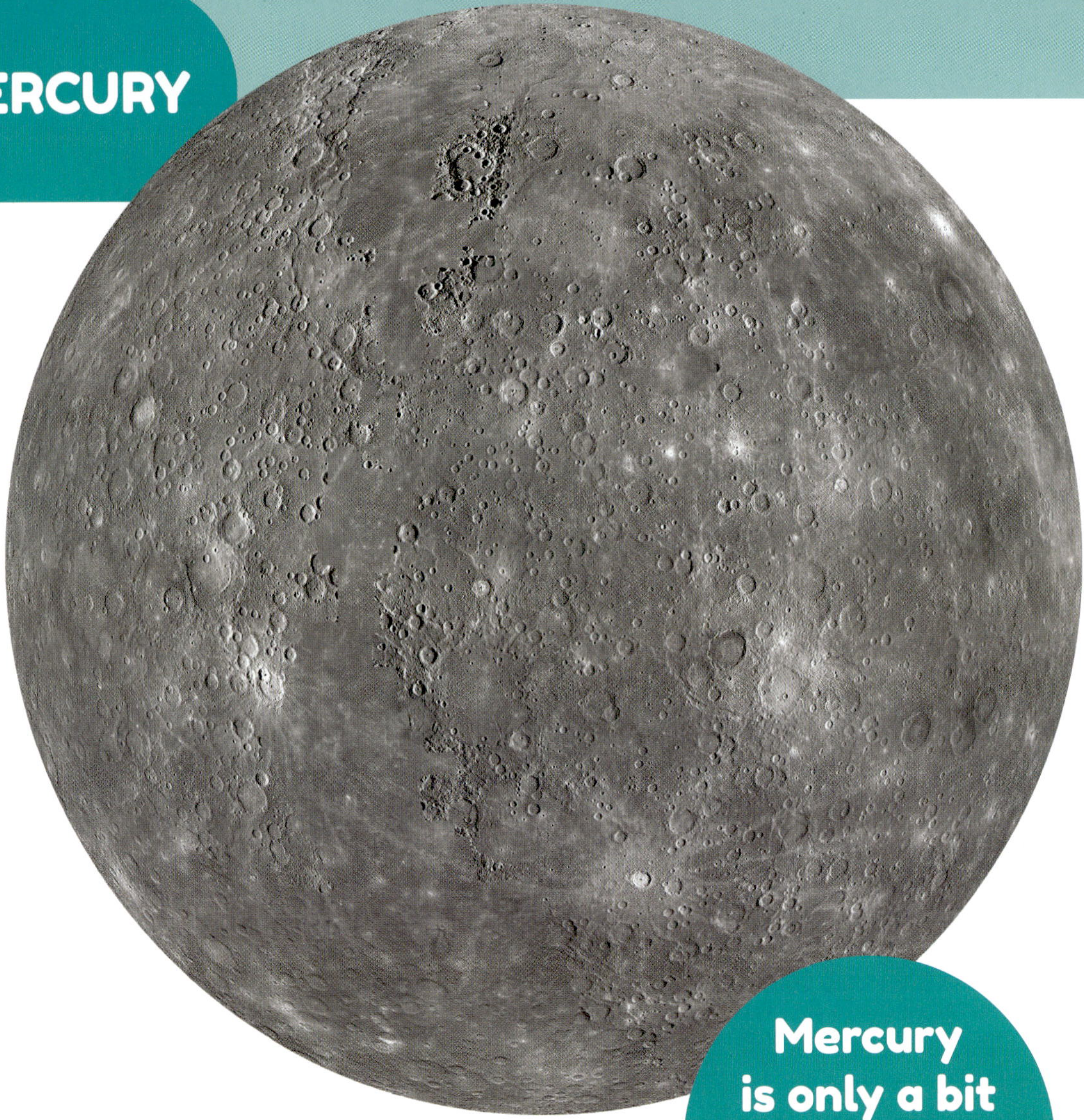

Mercury is only a bit bigger than Earth's Moon.

Closest to the Sun

Mercury is the closest planet to the Sun. It is only 36 million miles (58 million km) away. That makes the Sun 11 times brighter on Mercury than on Earth.

Size

Mercury is the smallest planet. It is 3,032 miles (4,880 km) wide. That is about one-third the size of Earth.

Mercury's Size Compared with Earth

If Earth were a nickel, Mercury would be a blueberry.

Sometimes Mercury crosses between Earth and the Sun. Several photos combined show its path against the Sun.

Fastest Year

Mercury has the shortest year. It completes an orbit around the Sun every 88 Earth days. Mercury spins slowly on its axis. One full spin equals one day on a planet. A day on Mercury takes 58.6 Earth days.

Extreme Temperatures

Mercury's long days and closeness to the Sun mean the surface has extreme temperatures. It can get as hot as 800 degrees Fahrenheit (430°C) during the day. The coldest temperatures are at night. They can reach about –290 degrees Fahrenheit (–180°C).

A colorized image shows Mercury's surface. The hotter parts are red. The green and blue parts are cooler.

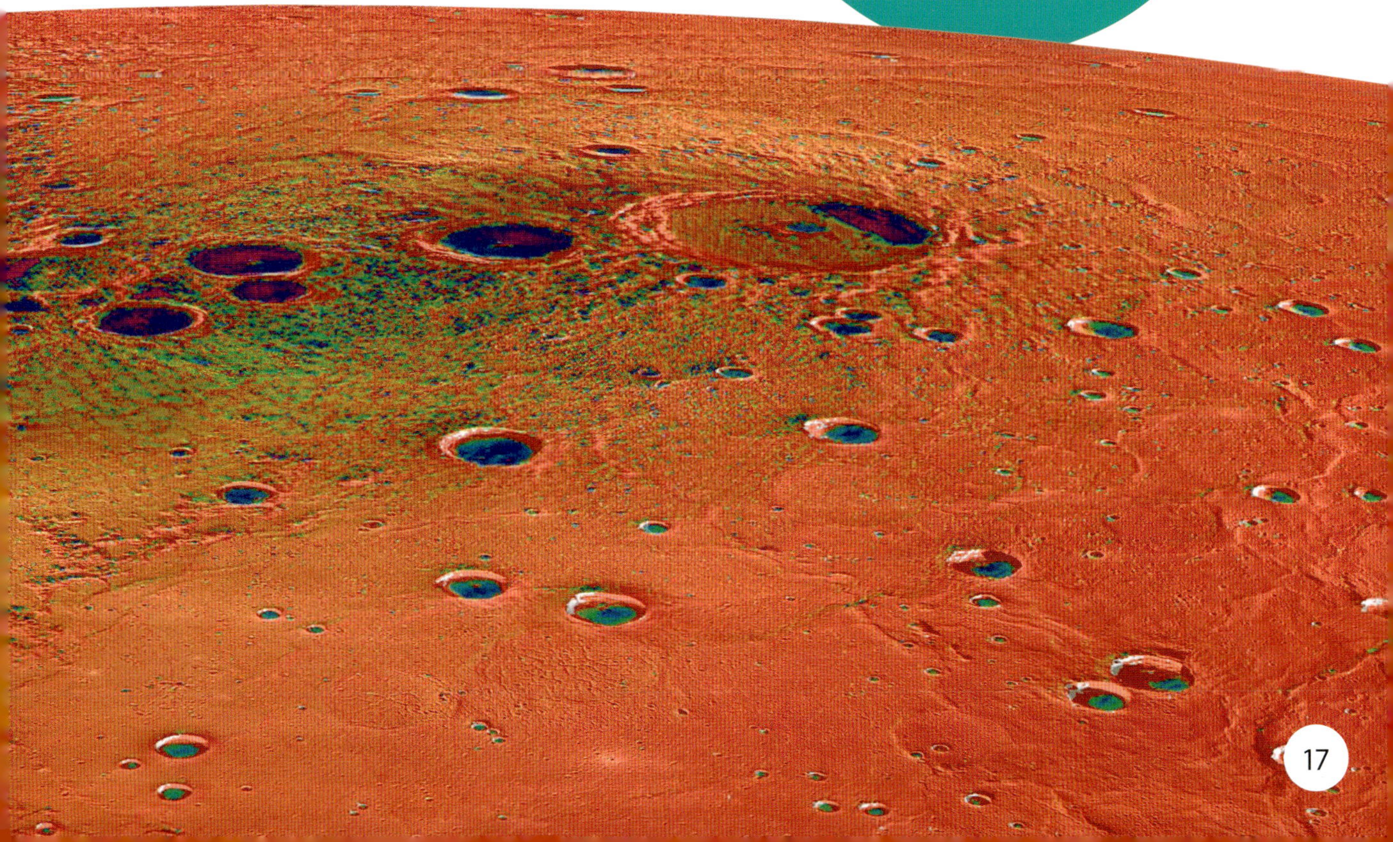

Surface

Mercury has a rocky surface. It is gray. It has many craters. The surface looks similar to Earth's Moon.

No Life

Living creatures need water and an atmosphere to survive. There is no atmosphere on Mercury. It has a thin exosphere. An exosphere is made of particles that stir up when solar wind or objects hit the surface. There also is no water. Scientists do not think there is any life on the planet.

Some of Mercury's craters have names, such as Enwonwu.

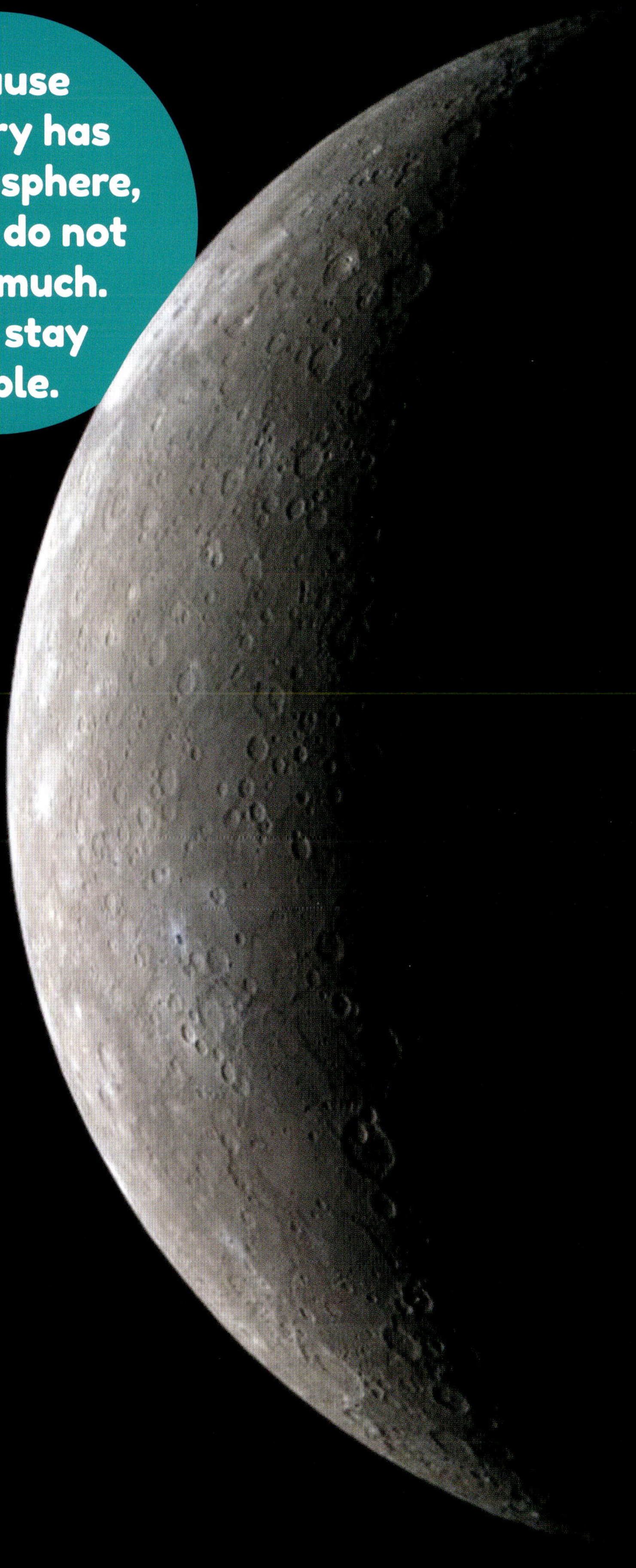

Because Mercury has no atmosphere, craters do not erode much. They stay visible.

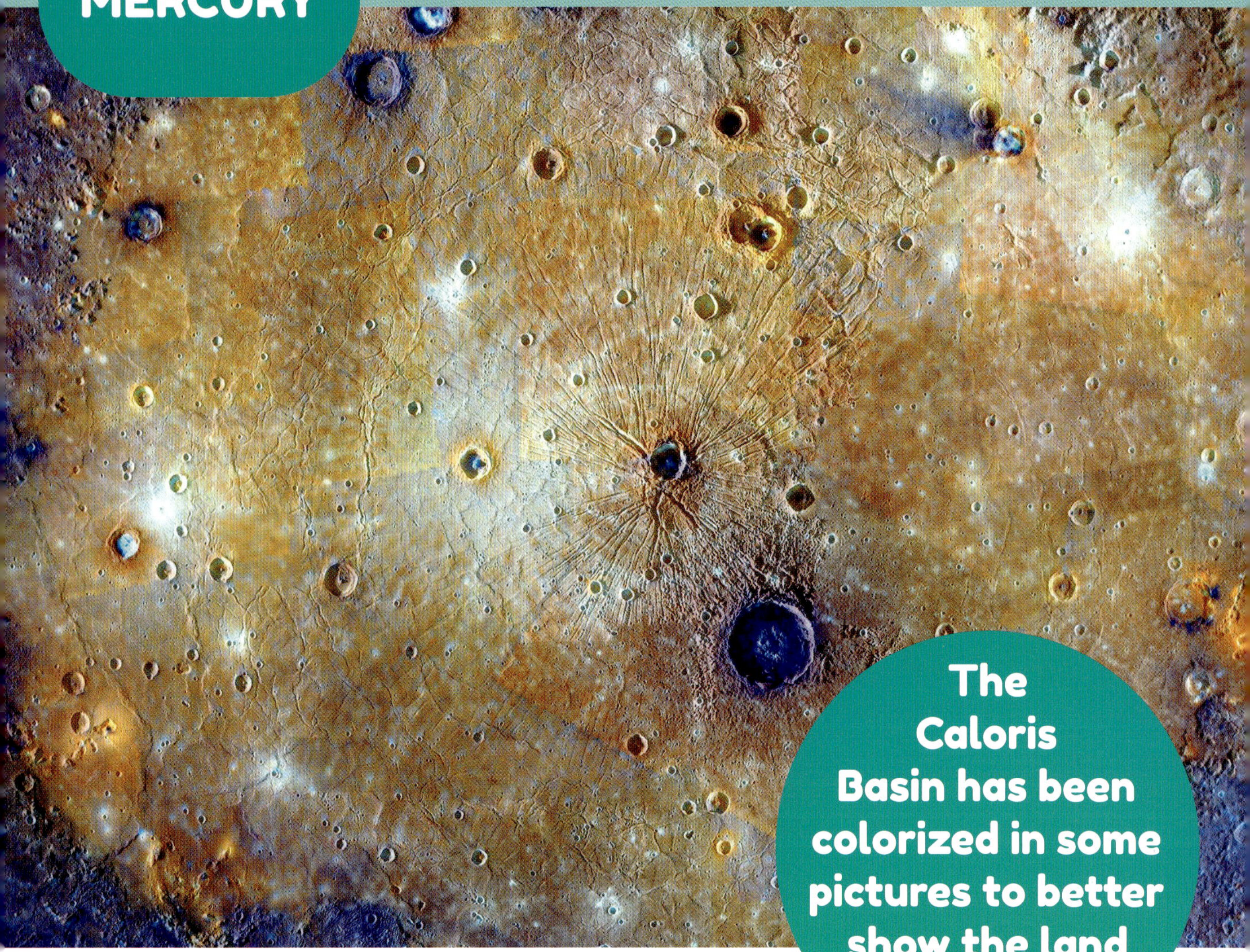

The Caloris Basin has been colorized in some pictures to better show the land features.

Features

Mercury has many large craters. The biggest is the Caloris Basin. An asteroid created it. The Caloris Basin is wider than Texas. Mercury has no rings. It does not have any moons.

Core

Mercury has a hot metal core, or center. Mercury's core has been cooling for billions of years. As it cooled, it made large cliffs on the surface. Some of them are a mile (1.6 km) high.

An artist depicts Mercury's layers. Its core makes up 85 percent of the planet's width.

Exploring Mercury

NASA's *Mariner 10* launched on November 3, 1973. It was the first spacecraft to study Mercury. The probe took nearly five months to reach Mercury. It found that Mercury had extreme temperatures and no atmosphere. It took more than 2,700 pictures of Mercury's surface.

FUN FACT!

Most planets are named for ancient Roman gods. Mercury was the messenger god.

Mariner 10 **used the pull of Venus's gravity to send it toward Mercury.**

An artist depicted *MESSENGER* studying Mercury.

MESSENGER

MESSENGER launched in August 2004. It flew by Venus once in 2006 and once in 2007. It reached Mercury in 2008. *MESSENGER* did three flybys. Then it orbited Mercury from 2011 to 2015. It studied what the planet was made of.

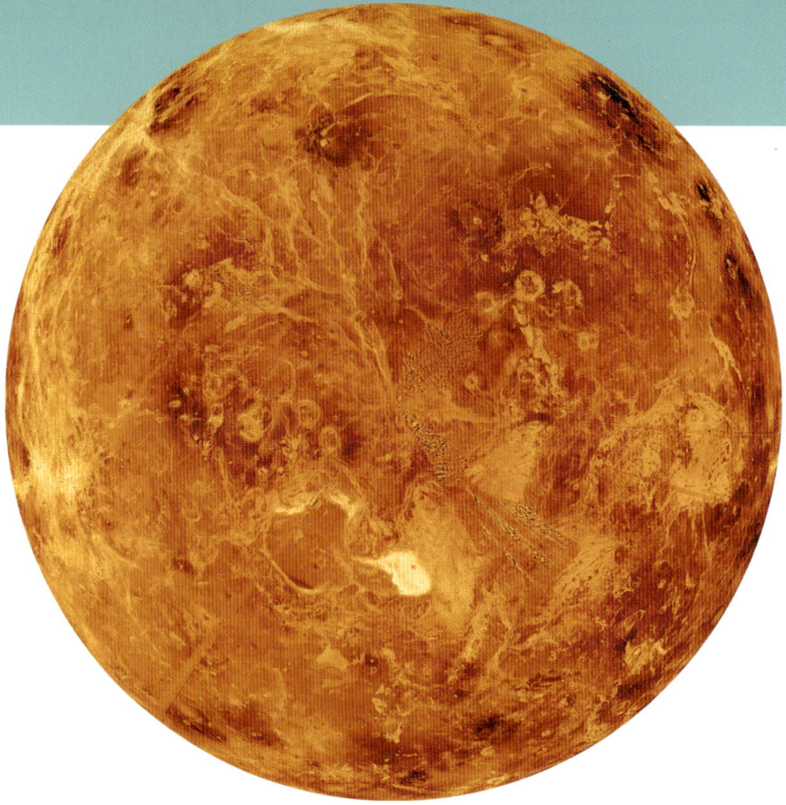

NASA's *Magellan* spacecraft took photos of Venus's northern half in 1996.

Location

Venus is the second-closest planet to the Sun. It is 67 million miles (108 million km) from the Sun. Venus's orbit is the closest to Earth's. The planet is close enough to see with the naked eye at night.

Long Days

A year on Venus lasts 224.7 Earth days. However, the planet spins more slowly than it orbits. One day on Venus takes 243 Earth days. This means its day lasts longer than its year. Venus has the longest day in the solar system.

Venus is called the Morning Star because it is often seen in the early morning.

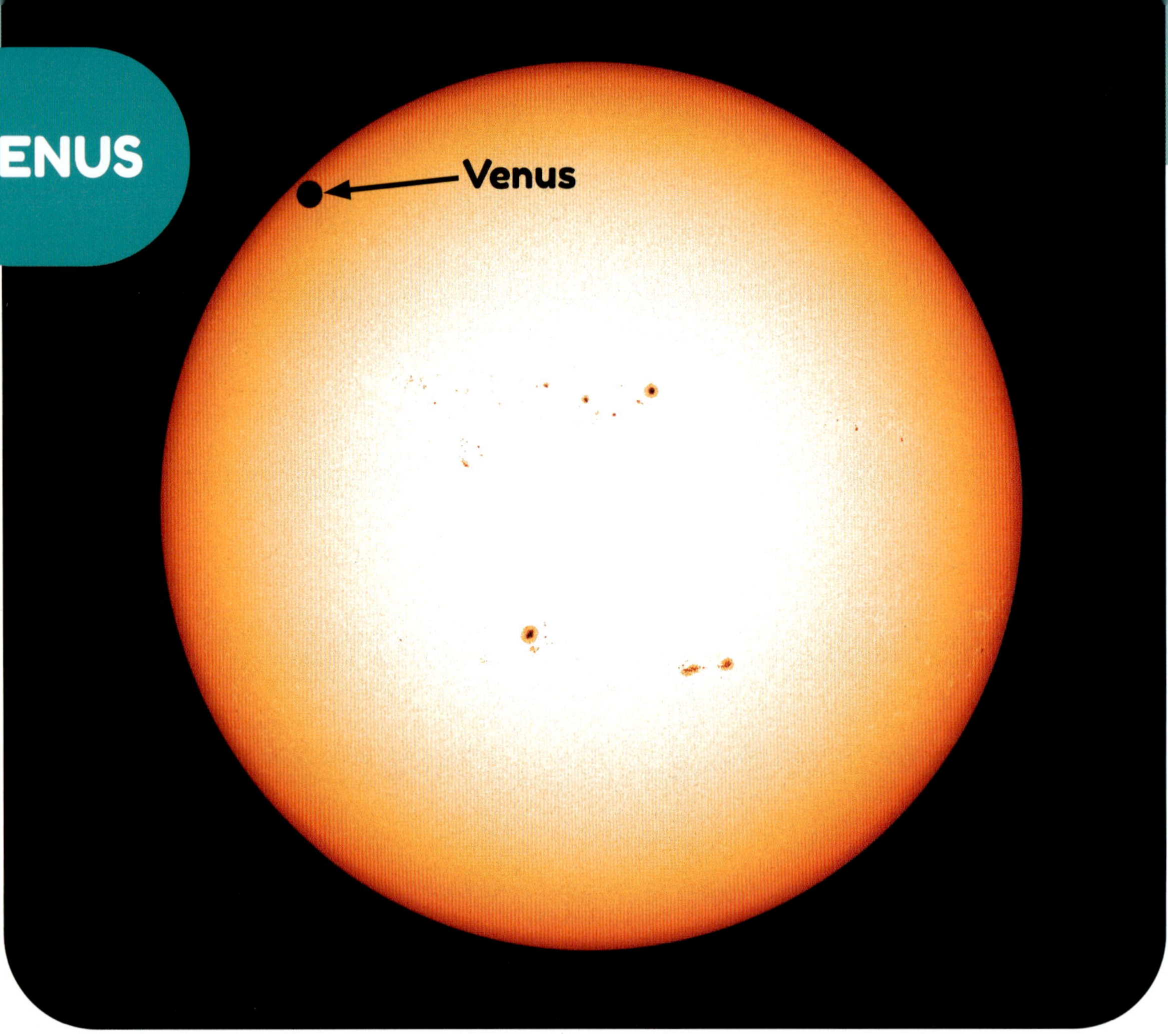

Sometimes Venus passes between Earth and the Sun. This is called a transit.

Backward Rotation

Venus spins clockwise. Clockwise means the direction hands move around a clock. Most planets spin in the other direction. Scientists think that a large object hit Venus. That made Venus start spinning in a different direction.

Earth's Twin

Venus is almost the same size as Earth. Earth is 7,926 miles (12,756 km) across. Venus is 7,521 miles (12,104 km) across. That's a difference of only 405 miles (652 km). People call Venus Earth's twin.

Venus's Size Compared with Earth

Venus is almost as wide as Earth.

Venus

Earth

Thick Atmosphere

Venus's atmosphere is heavy. The air pressure in Venus's atmosphere is 90 times stronger than Earth's atmosphere. That's the same pressure found 0.6 miles (1 km) under Earth's ocean. The thick atmosphere traps heat. This makes Venus the hottest planet in the solar system. It can reach 900 degrees Fahrenheit (482°C).

Venus's atmosphere is so thick the planet's surface cannot be seen from space.

Long Ago

Billions of years ago, Venus might have had water. At that time, the Sun was smaller. Venus was farther from it. About 700 million years ago, the Sun grew. Its surface was closer to Venus. Its heat made Venus's water evaporate. Venus was covered in heavy, heat-trapping clouds.

Surface

Venus has a rocky surface. It has at least 85,000 volcanoes. Some of these volcanoes still erupt. Venus also has large regions called terrae. Ishtar Terra is the size of Australia. Aphrodite Terra is the size of South America.

Exploring Venus

Humans have sent about 40 probes to Venus. About half of them have been successful. One was *Magellan*. NASA launched this probe on May 4, 1989. *Magellan* mapped the whole surface of Venus.

***Magellan* was built in Colorado.**

Akatsuki

Japan launched the *Akatsuki* probe on May 21, 2010. But an engine failed. The probe missed Venus. It orbited the Sun for five years.

***Akatsuki* means "Dawn" in Japanese.**

Akatsuki took photos of Venus.

Second Try

In 2015 *Akatsuki* got close enough to Venus to try again. Scientists used the probe's other engines to move *Akatsuki*. It reached orbit around Venus. The probe studies the planet's atmosphere.

Venera 7

In 1970 the Soviet Union's *Venera 7* probe landed on Venus. It became the first to land on another planet and send data back to Earth.

Earth is sometimes called the Blue Marble.

Location

Earth is the third planet from the Sun. It is 93 million miles (150 million km) from the Sun. Humans live on Earth. It's the only planet in the solar system that scientists know can support life.

A Day

Earth spins once every 23 hours and 56 minutes. This is one day. One Earth year is about 365 Earth days long.

Earth's orbit is not perfectly circular. Sometimes it is closer to the Sun, and other times it is farther away.

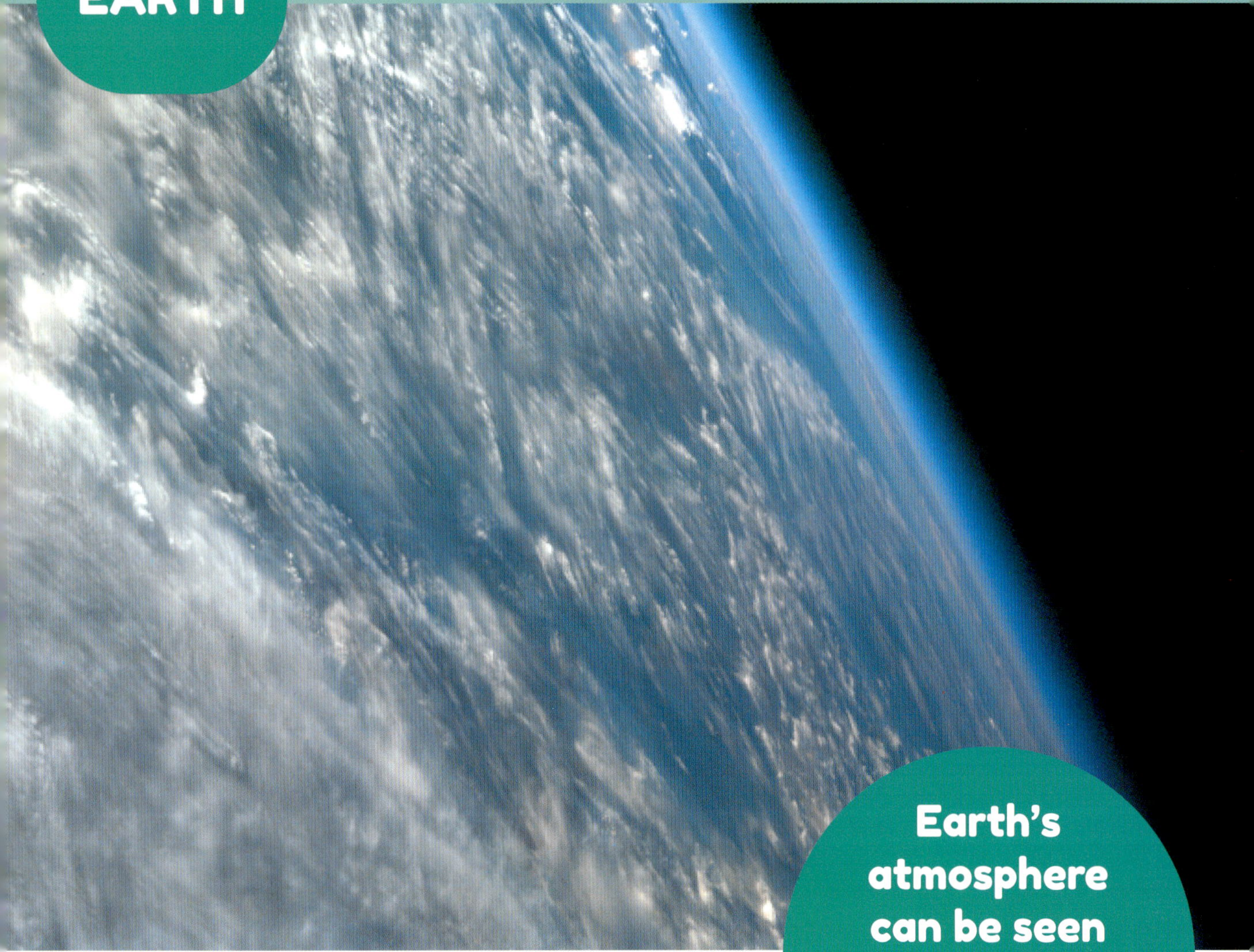

Earth's atmosphere can be seen from space as a blue haze above the surface.

Atmosphere

Earth's atmosphere is key for life. The atmosphere is made mostly of nitrogen. Twenty-one percent is oxygen. This is the gas that humans and other animals breathe.

Ozone

The atmosphere has a layer of ozone. This gas blocks a lot of the Sun's ultraviolet (UV) light. Too much UV light can hurt living things. It can cause cancer. Humans use sunscreen to help block UV light not stopped by the ozone layer.

Goldilocks Zone

Earth is at the right distance from the Sun for water to remain liquid. Scientists sometimes refer to this ideal range as the Goldilocks Zone.

People should use sunscreen with a sun protection factor (SPF) of at least 30.

Meteor Crater in Arizona was made about 50,000 years ago.

Earth's Surface

Earth is a rocky planet. It has many craters. The best-known is in Mexico. A meteorite hit there 66 million years ago. It made so much air pollution that sunlight couldn't reach Earth for years. This made Earth colder. The cold temperatures may have killed the dinosaurs.

Earth's Layers

Earth is made of four layers. At the very center is the inner core. It is made of solid metal. The outer core is liquid metal. The next layer is the mantle. The mantle is melted rock. The top layer is the crust. It is made of solid rock. It slides slowly on top of the mantle.

Earth's Layers

Earth has four main layers.

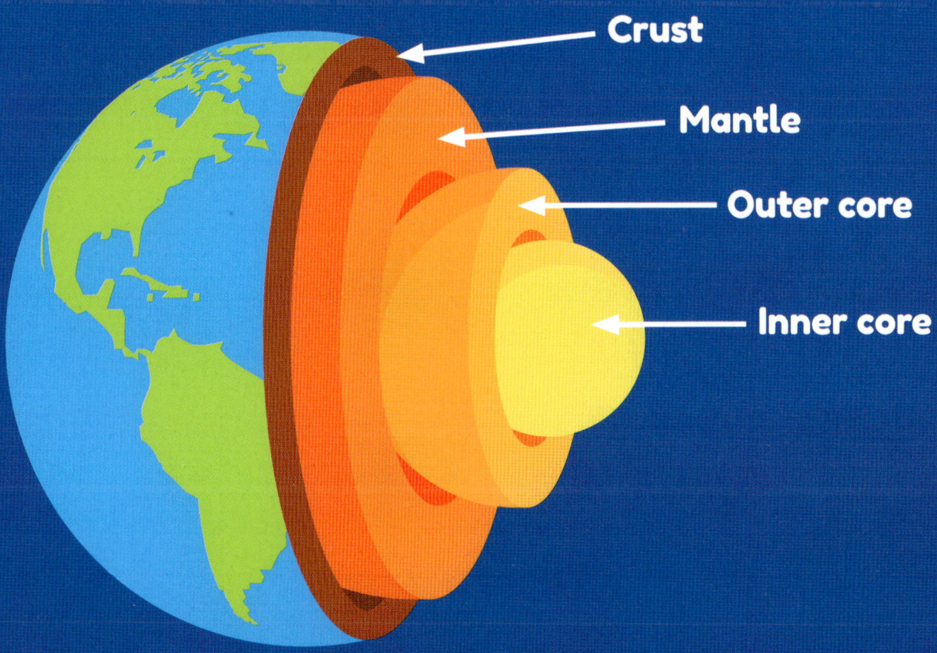

When parts of the crust hit each other, they push some land up high.

Earthquakes

Sometimes, different parts of the crust run into each other. This causes earthquakes. It also makes mountains form.

Water

All living things need water. Water covers 71 percent of Earth's surface. Only 3 percent is drinkable water. The rest is salt water. But that 3 percent is enough for all life on Earth.

Rivers are one type of freshwater source. People drink fresh water.

Pale Blue Dot

Some spacecraft take pictures of Earth. The *Voyager 1* probe took one of the most famous pictures in 1990. It took the photo from the edge of the solar system. In it, Earth is just a tiny speck. Astronomer Carl Sagan called Earth a "pale blue dot." This became the name of the photo.

In *Pale Blue Dot*, Earth is visible in the right sunray.

William Anders was on the Apollo 8 spacecraft when he took *Earthrise.*

Earthrise

Astronauts have taken pictures much closer to home. William Anders was in the Moon's orbit in 1968. He took a photo of the Moon's horizon. Earth is in the distance. This photo is called *Earthrise*.

Mars was named after the Roman god of war. The planet's red color reminded people of blood.

Location and Size

Mars is the fourth planet from the Sun. It is about 142 million miles (229 million km) from the Sun. Its high temperatures can reach 70 degrees Fahrenheit (21°C). At its coldest, Mars is –225 degrees Fahrenheit (–143°C). Mars is about half the width of Earth.

Matching Days

A day on Mars is 24 hours and 37 minutes. It is only a little longer than an Earth day. The year is much longer. Mars takes 687 Earth days to go around the Sun.

Mars's Size Compared with Earth

If Earth were a nickel, Mars would be a small marble.

Moons

Mars has two moons. The largest is Phobos. It is 17 miles (27 km) across. Deimos is smaller at only 9 miles (14 km) across.

Phobos circles around Mars three times each day.

The Hubble Space Telescope took several photos that tracked Phobos's orbit around Mars.

Shape

Mars's moons are not round like Earth's Moon. They are lumpy. They look like rocks someone might pick up off the ground.

MARS

The *Phoenix* Mars lander took true color photos of Mars's ground.

The Red Planet

Mars looks red from far away. This color comes from iron in the rocks and soil. Wind kicks up the red dirt. That makes the whole planet look red from afar. Up close, Mars has brown and golden colors too.

Life on Mars?

Scientists are looking for evidence of life on Mars. That life would be smaller than the eye can see. It might live under the ice caps or in frozen lakes.

Water on Mars

Scientists have identified water on Mars. The planet has 1.2 million cubic miles (5 million cubic km) of ice. There might be liquid water below the surface.

Ice can be found near Mars's north pole.

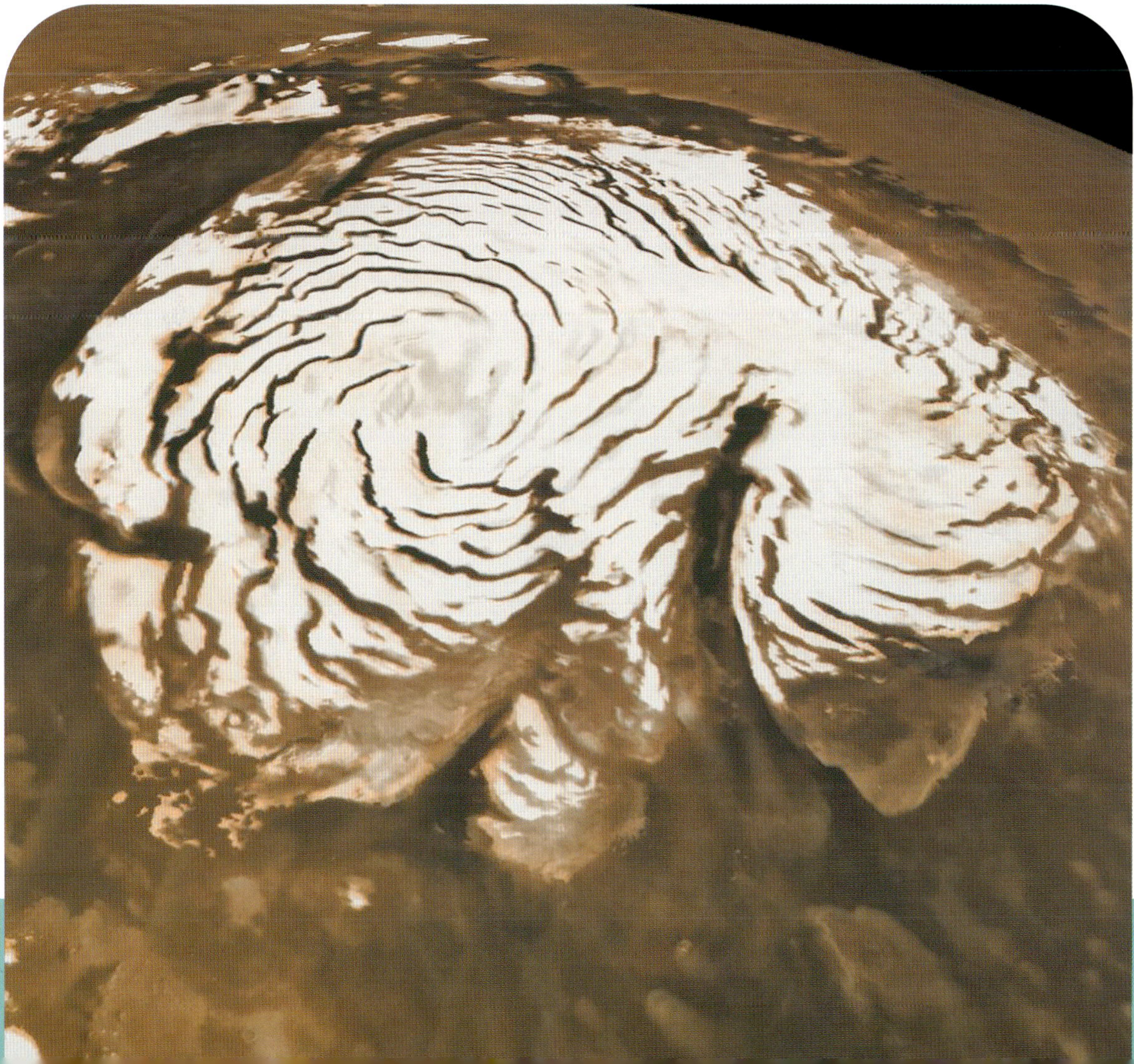

Volcano

Mars has the solar system's biggest volcano. It is named Olympus Mons. This volcano is three times as tall as Mount Everest, Earth's highest mountain. It rises 16 miles (26 km) above the surface. Scientists think the volcano could still be active.

FUN FACT!

On Mars, earthquakes are called Marsquakes.

Olympus Mons is as wide as France.

Valles Marineris is more than 200 miles (320 km) wide at parts.

Canyon

Valles Marineris is a canyon unlike any on Earth. It is about 3,000 miles (4,800 km) long. That is as long as the entire United States. It is up to 4 miles (7 km) deep. Scientists think Mars was once hot. As it cooled, the crust cracked. This crack became the canyon.

In 1965 the *Mariner 4* probe took the first close images of Mars.

Exploring Mars

NASA sent several probes to Mars in the 1960s. The Mariner missions had many successes. But there were also some failures. Researchers learned how to make better probes.

The Rovers

Some robots land on Mars. They are called rovers. These rovers travel over the surface. They collect soil samples. They run experiments. The first Mars rover landed in 1997. In 2023 there were two active rovers. They were named *Curiosity* and *Perseverance*.

The *Ingenuity* helicopter arrived with *Perseverance* in 2021.

JUPITER

Jupiter is named after the king of the Roman gods because of its large size.

Location

Jupiter is the fifth planet from the Sun. It was the first planet to form in the solar system. It is 483 million miles (777 million km) away from the Sun.

Size

Jupiter is the largest planet in the solar system. It is 86,881 miles (139,821 km) wide. Jupiter could hold more than 1,300 Earths.

Jupiter's Size Compared with Earth

If Earth were the size of a nickel, Jupiter would be the size of a basketball.

Length of Day

Jupiter's days are only ten hours long. The years are much longer. It takes the planet 12 Earth years to orbit once around the Sun.

Jupiter has several layers. Astronomers are unsure whether its core is solid.

Gas Giant

Jupiter is a gas giant. It is made mostly of hydrogen gas. Because Jupiter is so big, gases near its center are under a lot of pressure. They turn into liquid. This means Jupiter has the largest ocean in the solar system. It is made of liquid hydrogen instead of water.

FUN FACT!

Jupiter has faint rings. Astronomers discovered them in the 1970s.

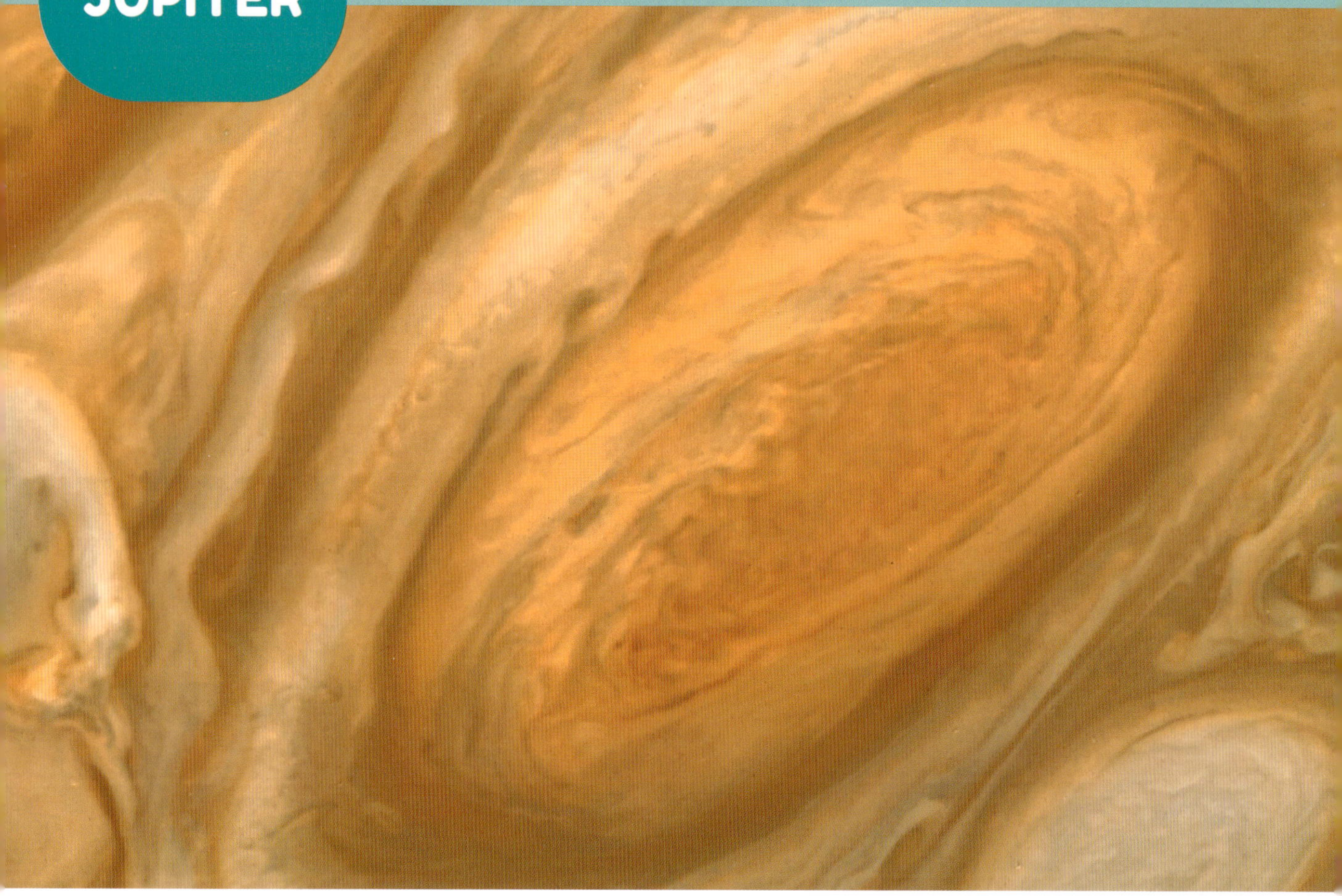

The Great Red Spot is a swirl of storm clouds.

The Great Red Spot

Jupiter is known for its Great Red Spot. This spot is a giant storm that has lasted at least 150 years. Today it is slightly bigger than Earth. But it is shrinking. In the late 1800s, it was about three times as big as Earth.

Io

Jupiter has 95 moons. One of them is Io. This moon has hundreds of active volcanoes. Jupiter's strong gravity causes Io's crust to stretch. Then the crust relaxes. That makes sections of the crust rub against each other. It can get hot enough to melt rock into magma. The magma erupts from volcanoes.

Europa

Europa is another moon of Jupiter. It is the smoothest object in the solar system. It has hardly any craters or mountains. This means Europa is probably younger than other moons. There has been less time for objects to hit it.

Several photos were combined to make a full photo of Europa.

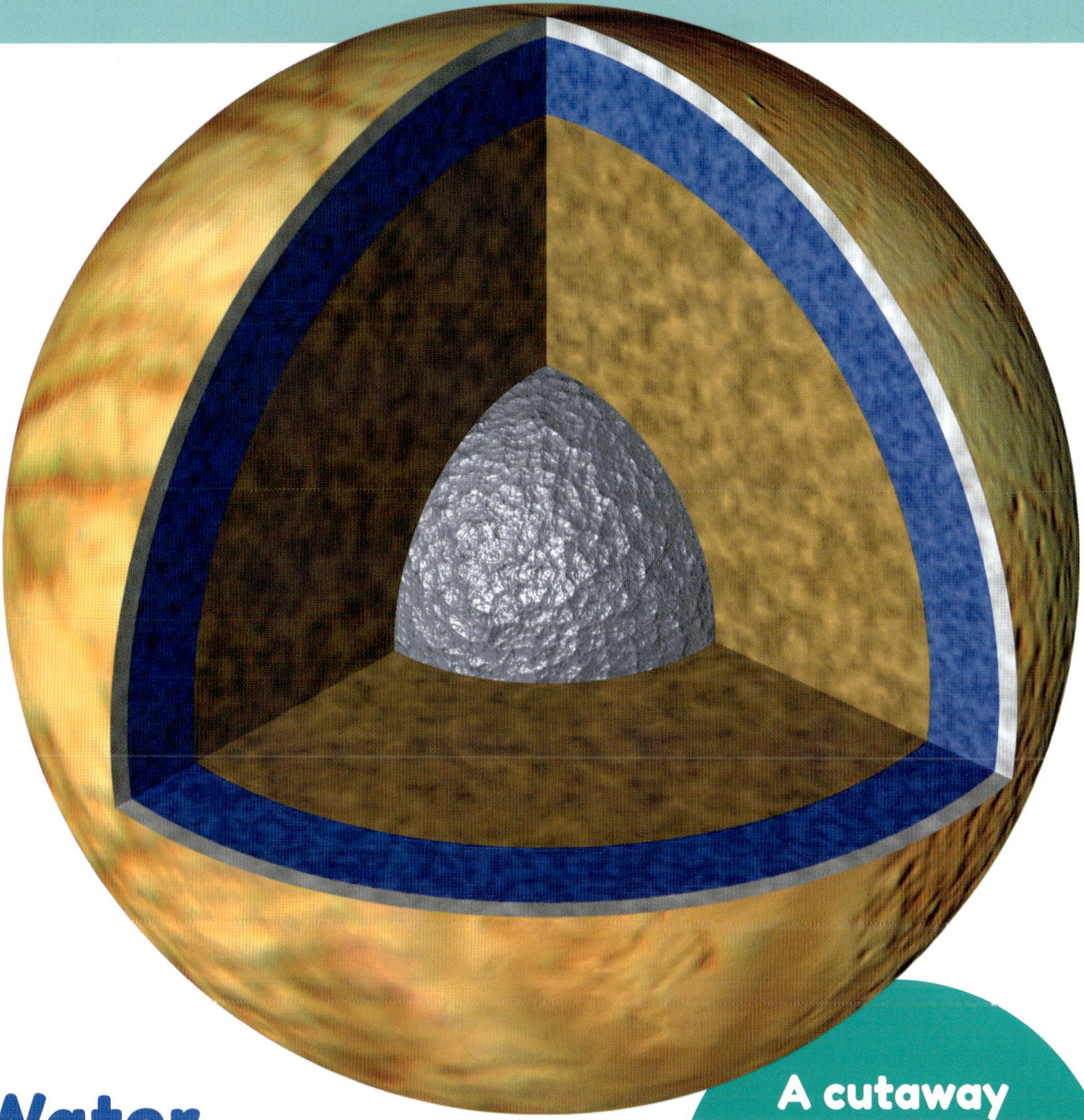

A cutaway shows Europa's possible layers, including water, *blue*.

Water

Europa is covered in ice. Researchers think that a huge watery ocean lies under the surface. It may hold twice as much water as Earth's oceans.

An artist depicted *Galileo* leaving Earth in 1989.

Exploring Jupiter

NASA launched the *Galileo* orbiter on October 18, 1989. *Galileo* studied Jupiter's moons. It was the first to determine that Europa has salt water. It studied Io's volcanos.

Juice

The European Space Agency launched the *Jupiter Icy Moons Explorer* (*Juice*) probe on April 14, 2023. It was being sent to the moons Europa, Callisto, and Ganymede. Its mission was to find out if life can form on the moons.

Galileo Galilei

Galileo Galilei was an astronomer in the 1600s. He used a telescope to study the Moon's craters and mountains. He also discovered Jupiter's moons.

Artwork shows *Juice* alongside Jupiter and one of the planet's moons.

Location

Saturn is the sixth planet away from the Sun. It is about 886 million miles (1.4 billion km) from the Sun.

Saturn is nine times Earth's width, not including its rings.

It takes 80 minutes for sunlight to reach Saturn.

Size and Day

Saturn is the second-biggest planet in the solar system. It is 72,367 miles (116,463 km) across. More than 760 Earths could fit inside. The planet's day lasts only 10.7 hours. But one year on Saturn is 29.4 Earth years.

Each of Saturn's rings orbits the planet at a different speed.

The Rings

Sometimes space objects hit each other. They break into pieces. Saturn's rings are made of these pieces. Some are as big as houses. There are seven main rings.

Many More Rings

Saturn has the most visible rings in the solar system. But Jupiter, Uranus, and Neptune also have rings.

Windy Planet

Saturn is a gas giant. It looks mostly brown, yellow, and gray. The planet's winds can blow as hard as 1,090 miles per hour (1,750 kmh). That is 4.5 times faster than a hurricane on Earth.

Saturn's Size Compared with Earth

If Saturn were a volleyball, Earth would be a nickel.

Saturn's Moons

Saturn has 145 moons. That is the most moons of any planet. Some of those moons are as far as 18 million miles (29 million km) away from the planet.

The first moon of Saturn to be discovered was Titan in 1655.

Some of Saturn's moons, such as Prometheus, lie between the planet's rings.

Catching Moons

Saturn's size and age helped it gain so many moons. Saturn formed before many other planets. It had stronger gravity than most solar system objects at the time. So it pulled large objects into its orbit.

The surface temperature of Titan is –290 degrees Fahrenheit (–179°C).

Titan

Titan is Saturn's largest moon. It is bigger than Mercury. This moon has liquid on its surface. But the liquid is not water. It is a chemical called methane.

Enceladus

Enceladus is another of Saturn's moons. It is as wide as Arizona. It has the most reflective surface in the solar system. It reflects almost all sunlight that hits it. The moon's surface is icy. Water and gas spray from cracks. Scientists think there is a large ocean under the icy surface.

Some of the material that sprays out of Enceladus becomes part of Saturn's rings.

Exploring Saturn

The *Cassini* probe launched toward Saturn on October 15, 1997. It orbited Saturn for more than ten years. It also carried a smaller probe called *Huygens*. *Huygens* landed on the surface of Titan. The surface was covered with pebbles of ice.

***Cassini* flew by Venus and Jupiter on its way to Saturn.**

An artist created an image showing *Dragonfly* on Titan.

Dragonfly

In 2019 NASA started planning a probe called *Dragonfly*. The probe would visit Titan. It would be a quadcopter drone. *Dragonfly* would land to take samples of the surface. The probe was scheduled to launch in 2027. It would reach Titan in 2034. Researchers hoped to see if life exists on Titan.

Uranus is the third-largest planet in the solar system, after Jupiter and Saturn.

Location and Size

Uranus (pronounced YUR-uh-nuhs) is the seventh planet from the Sun. It is 1.8 billion miles (2.9 billion km) away from the Sun. Uranus is 31,158 miles (50,144 km) across. That is four times wider than Earth.

Length of Day and Year

Uranus spins quickly. A day lasts 17 hours. The planet's orbit is much longer. A year on Uranus is 84 Earth years.

Uranus's Size Compared with Earth

If Uranus were a softball, Earth would be a nickel.

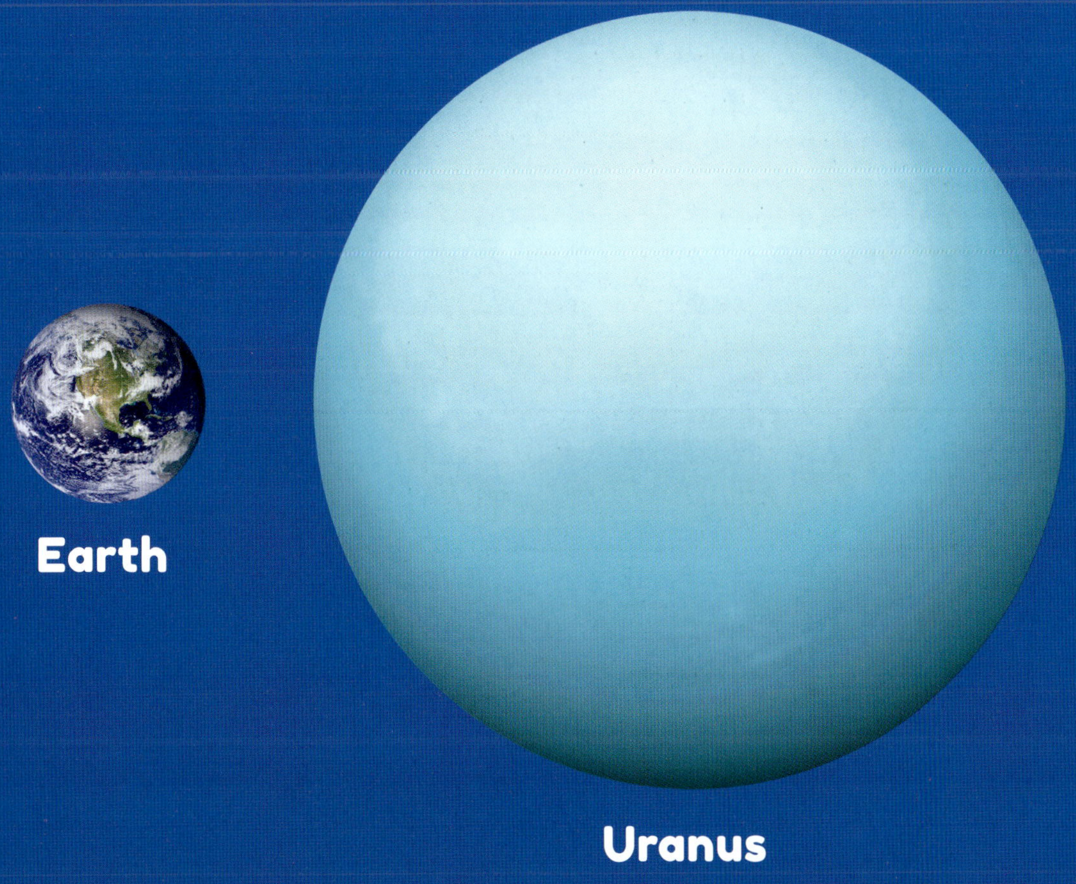

Atmosphere

Uranus is an ice giant. Ice giants have icy and rocky cores. Gas surrounds the core. One of Uranus's gases is methane. Methane gives Uranus an icy blue color. The atmosphere has high temperature and pressure. The heat and pressure are so high that it might rain diamonds.

Uranus's atmosphere circles the planet in the same direction the planet rotates.

Uranus's rings show the extreme tilt of the planet.

Rings and Tilt

Scientists think Uranus was hit by an Earth-sized object long ago. That caused Uranus to tilt on its side. The tilt is best seen in the rings. Uranus has two sets of rings. The rings circle the planet vertically. Other planets' rings circle horizontally.

FUN FACT!

Uranus is the only planet named for a Greek god.

Scientists think Uranus formed closer to the Sun and then moved farther away.

Extreme Cold

Uranus is the coldest planet in the solar system. Its atmosphere gets as cold as –372 degrees Fahrenheit (–224°C). Uranus is closer to the Sun than Neptune. But it is colder. Scientists think the collision that tilted Uranus may have made the planet lose its heat.

Rocky Core

Most gas giants don't have a solid surface. But Uranus likely has a rocky core beneath the clouds. The core may get as hot as 9,000 degrees Fahrenheit (5,000°C).

The core of Uranus has a little more than half the mass of Earth.

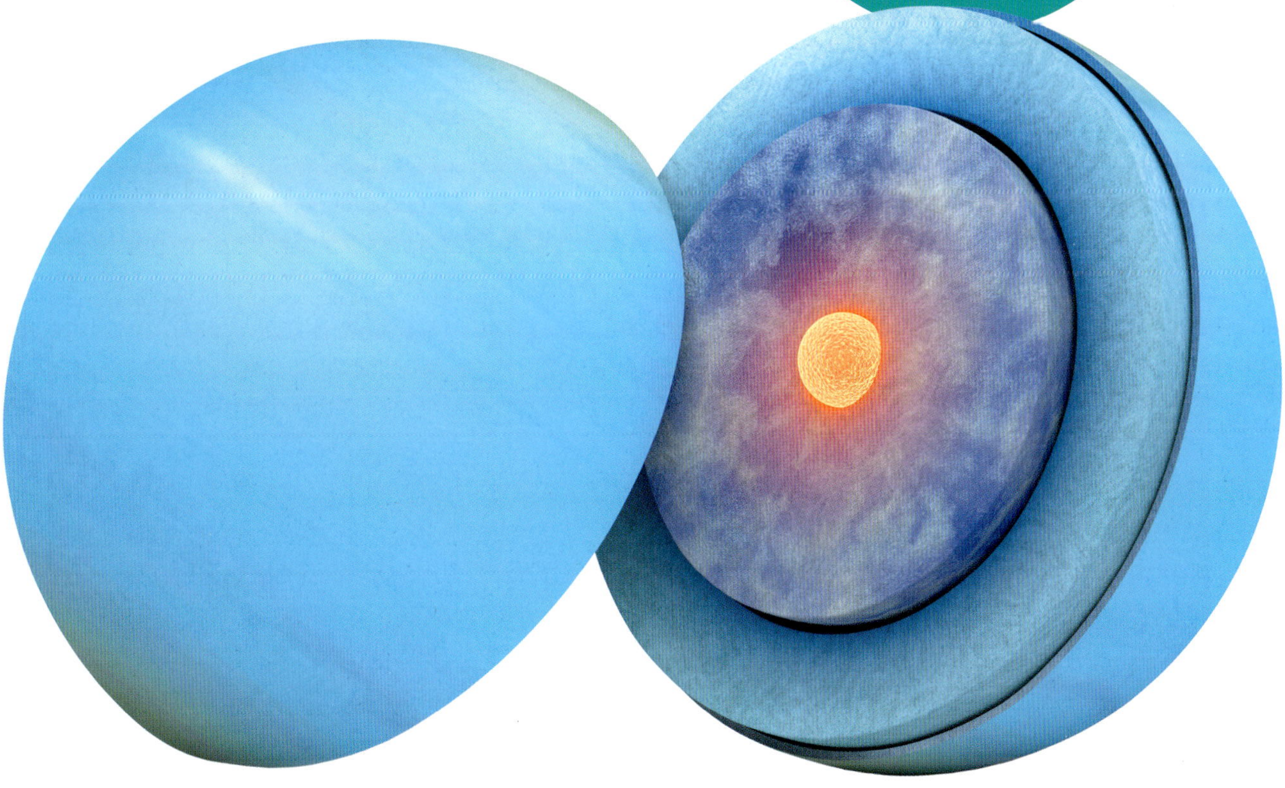

Uranus's Moons

Uranus has 27 moons. Miranda has canyons 12 times deeper than the Grand Canyon on Earth. Another moon, Oberon, has many craters. The craters are covered with dark material. Scientists do not know what the material is.

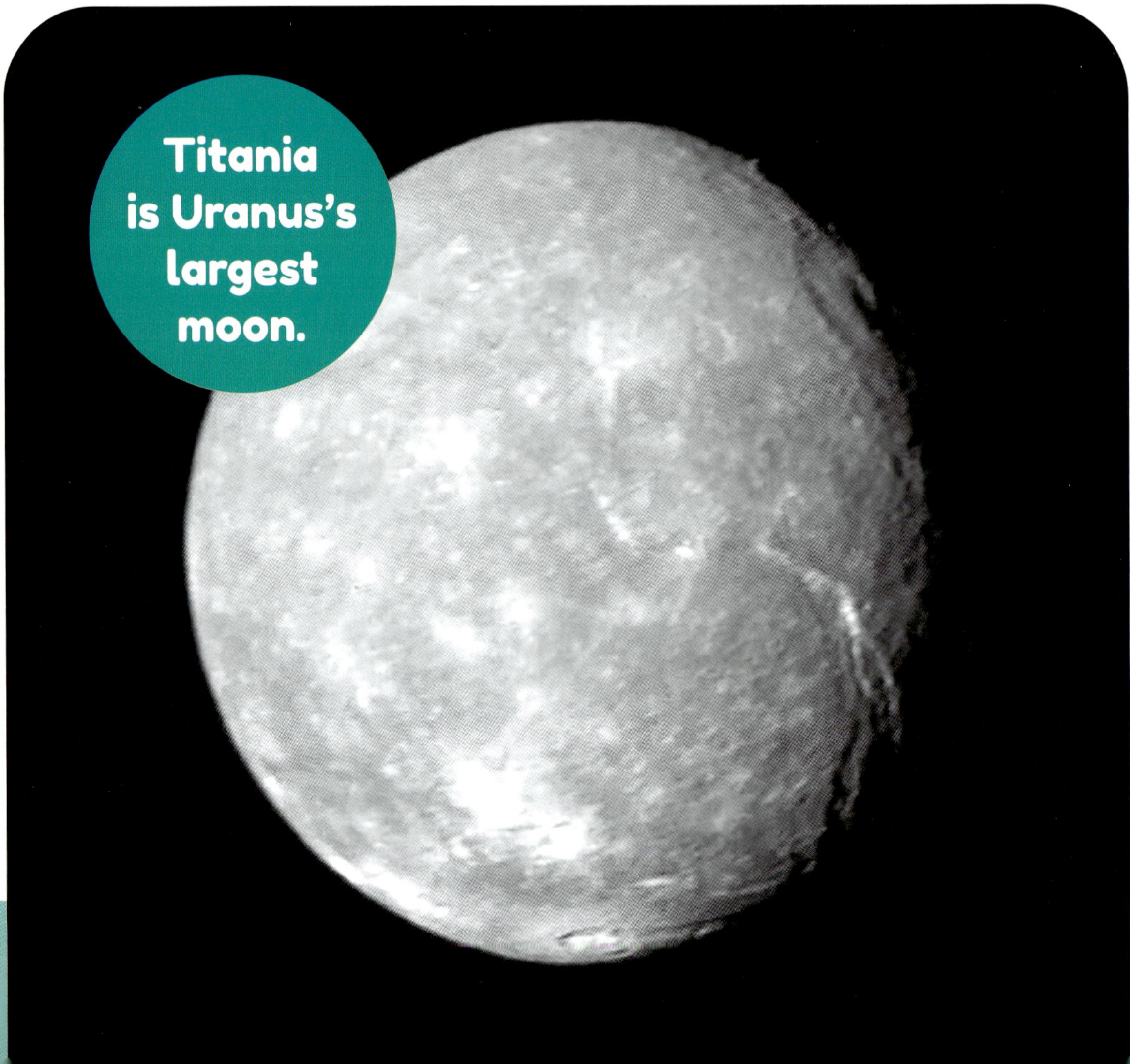

Titania is Uranus's largest moon.

Shepherd Moons

Cordelia and Ophelia are called shepherd moons. Between them are several smaller moons. Scientists think that Cordelia and Ophelia's gravity helps keep the shape of Uranus's farthest ring.

Character Moons

Uranus's moons are named after characters in plays by William Shakespeare and poems by Alexander Pope.

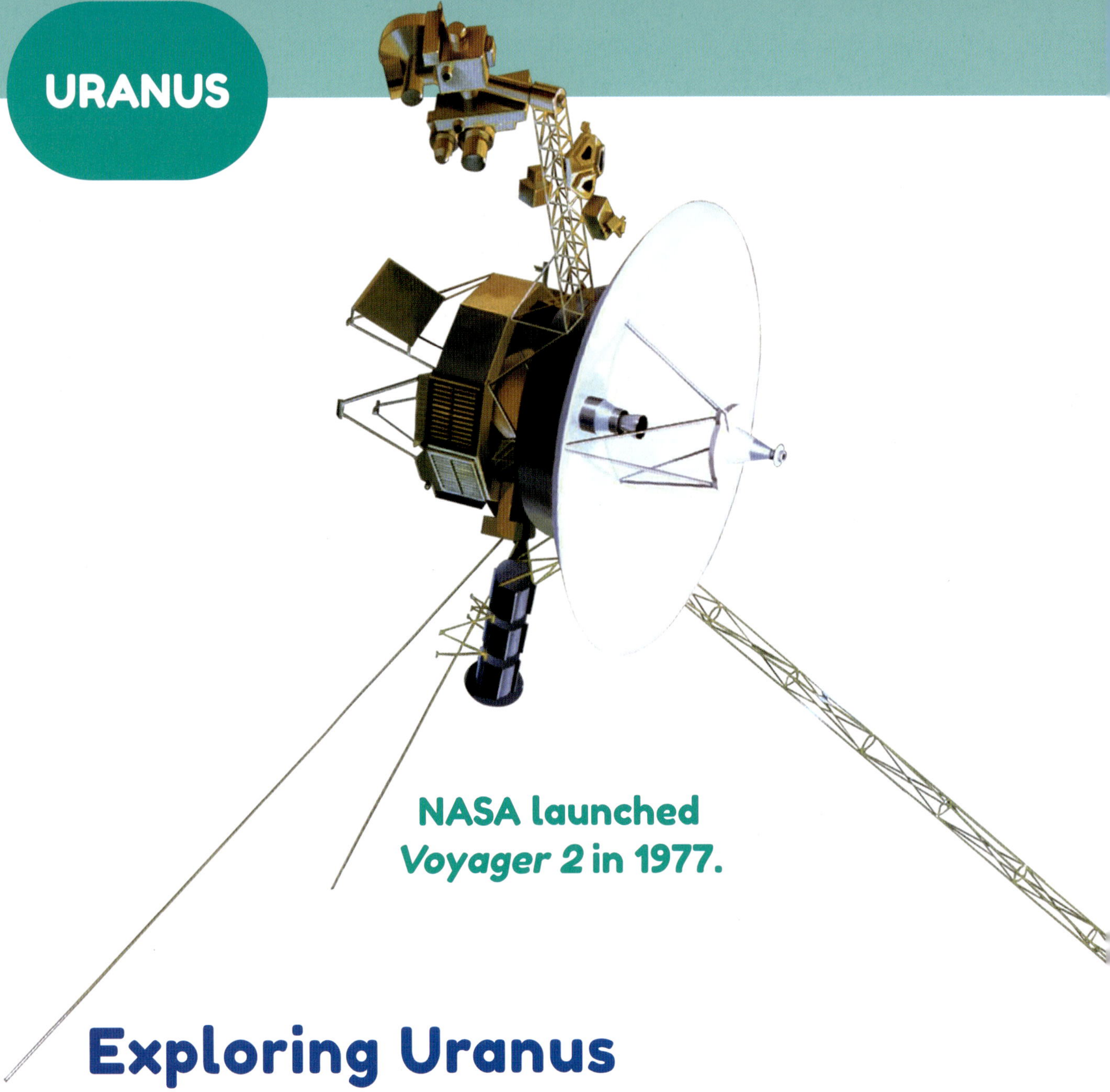

NASA launched *Voyager 2* in 1977.

Exploring Uranus

Only one probe has made it to Uranus. In 1986 *Voyager 2* flew near the planet. It studied the planet's atmosphere and core. It discovered 11 new moons.

Hubble Space Telescope

Powerful telescopes have gathered data on Uranus. One is the Hubble Space Telescope. Hubble has observed the planet's weather. It tracks a large storm that covers the entire north pole.

The Hubble Space Telescope can see objects better than telescopes on the ground because Earth's atmosphere is not in its way.

FUN FACT!

All of the solar system's planets could fit in the space between Earth and the Moon.

Neptune is named after the Roman god of the sea.

Location and Size

Neptune is the farthest planet from the Sun. It is 2.8 billion miles (4.5 billion km) away from the Sun. Sunlight takes four hours to reach the planet.

Size, Days, and Years

Neptune is 30,598 miles (49,243 km) across. It is only a bit smaller than Uranus. A day on Neptune takes only 16 Earth hours. It takes 165 Earth years to make one trip around the Sun.

Neptune's Size Compared with Earth

If Neptune were a softball, Earth would be a nickel.

Ice Giant

Neptune is known as an ice giant. Its gases include hydrogen, helium, and methane. Neptune's temperatures can drop to –360 degrees Fahrenheit (–220°C).

Neptune's core is about the size of Earth.

Blue Planet

Neptune and Uranus are blue because of methane gas. Neptune is a darker shade of blue. This is because it has more active weather. Uranus has slower winds. Neptune's storms mix the atmosphere and create a darker color.

FUN FACT!

Neptune has completed only one orbit since its discovery in 1846.

One of Neptune's largest storms is called the Great Dark Spot.

Big Storms

Neptune has the fastest winds in the solar system. They can get as fast as 1,500 miles per hour (2,400 kmh). The winds can create large storms. The storms appear as dark blue patches. Some storms are as wide as Earth.

Neso

Neptune has 14 moons. Neso is one. Its orbit is millions of miles away from the planet. Neso is the farthest moon from its planet. It might be the remains of a larger moon that broke up billions of years ago.

Neptune has rings, but they are very hard to see without special cameras.

Triton

Neptune's largest moon is Triton. It is a bit smaller than Earth's Moon. Triton is an icy moon. The same side of Triton always faces Neptune.

Triton has volcanoes.

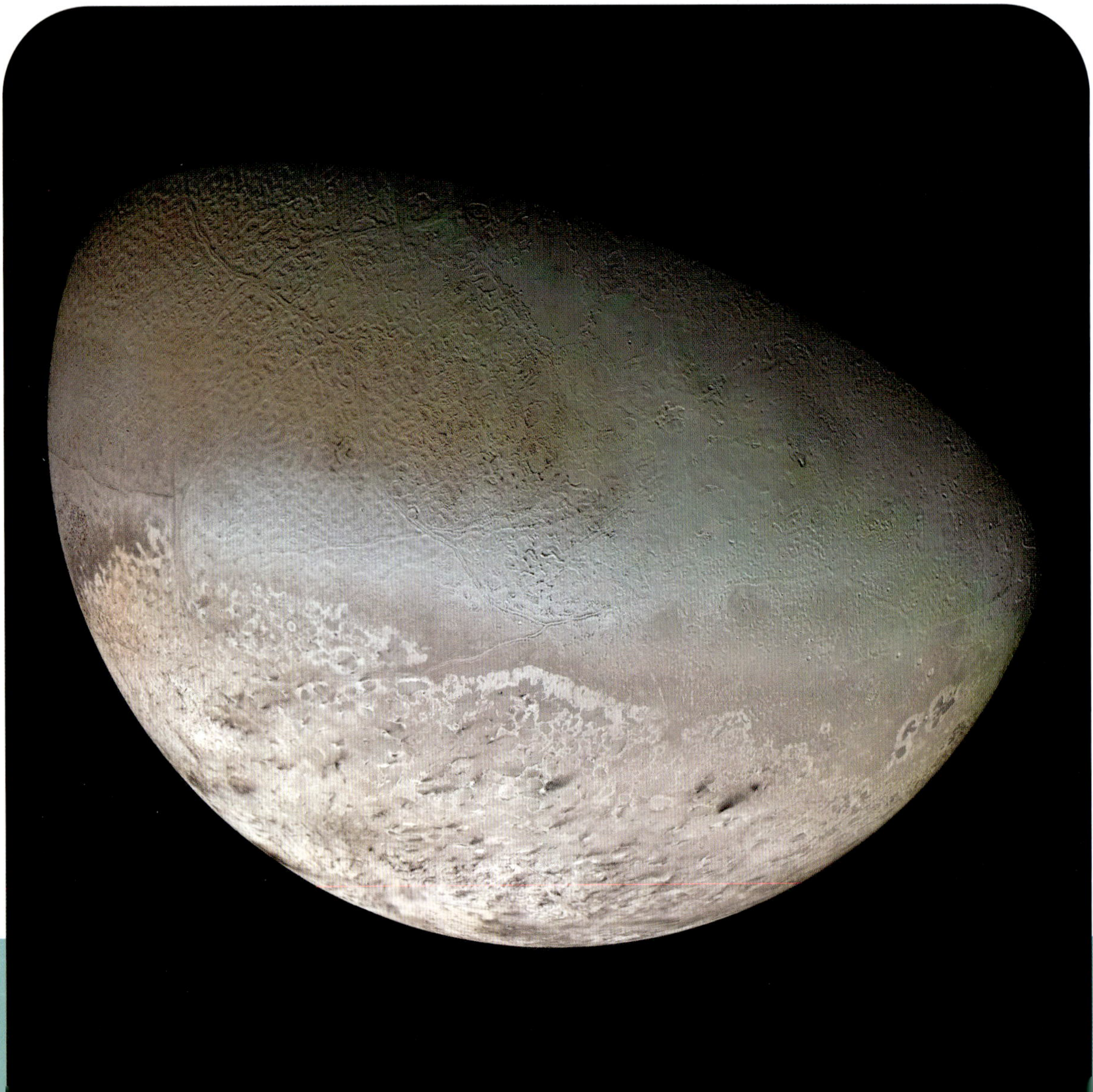

Triton, *bottom*, is slightly closer to Neptune than the Moon is to Earth.

Triton's Orbit

Triton orbits in the opposite direction of Neptune's spin. Neptune spins counterclockwise. Triton orbits it clockwise. Scientists think this is because Triton did not form at the same time as Neptune. Instead, it was a passing object. Neptune's gravity captured it.

After launching in 1977, *Voyager 2* flew out of the solar system in 2018.

Exploring Neptune

Voyager 2 is the only probe to visit Neptune. It reached the planet in 1989. The probe discovered six new moons and four rings. It took pictures of Triton.

Future Visits

Scientists search for planets around other stars. They find a lot of planets like Neptune. In the 2020s, researchers considered sending a new probe to Neptune. The mission would be called Neptune Odyssey. It might help astronomers understand why planets such as Neptune form.

One goal of the Neptune Odyssey mission was to study Triton.

The same side of the Moon always faces Earth.

Formation

Earth has one moon. It is simply called the Moon. Researchers think the Moon was formed at the same time as Earth. When Earth was forming, a Mars-sized object hit it. That object caused melted rocks to fly off Earth. Those rocks came together to make the Moon.

Tides

The Moon is 238,855 miles (384,450 km) away from Earth. The Moon is only one-third the width of Earth. But its gravity affects Earth. The Moon's gravity pulls at the ocean's waters. This causes Earth's tides, the rise and fall of sea levels.

The Moon's Size Compared with Earth

If Earth were a nickel, the Moon would be a pea.

Phases

The Moon goes through eight phases. When the Moon is between Earth and the Sun, it is called a new moon. It is hard to see. When it is a bright round shape in the sky, it's called a full moon. Earth is between the Sun and Moon. One complete cycle takes 29.5 days.

Phases of the Moon

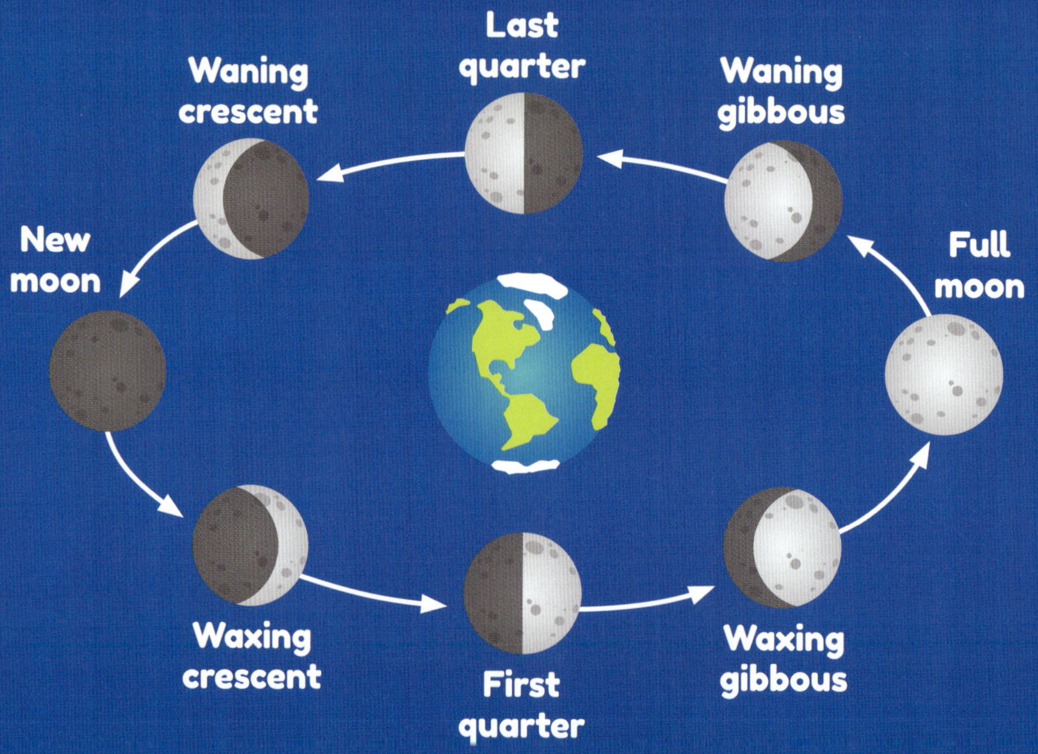

The Moon gets about 180 new craters each year.

Craters

The Moon has a rocky gray surface. It is covered in big and small craters. The biggest is the Aitken Basin. It is almost 5 miles (8 km) deep. A giant asteroid made the basin.

FUN FACT!

The Moon is drifting away from Earth by about 1.5 inches (3.8 cm) each year.

Reiner Gamma is a lunar swirl on the Moon's surface.

Lunar Swirls

The moon has bright marks. They are called lunar swirls. These marks are often wavy. They aren't found anywhere else in the solar system. Scientists believe magnetic moon rocks may cause the swirls.

FUN FACT!

The Moon has moonquakes caused by Earth's gravity.

Exploring the Moon

In the 1950s, the Soviet Union and the United States raced to the Moon. Both wanted to be the first to land a person on the moon. The United States won the race in 1969. US astronaut Neil Armstrong was the first person to walk on the Moon.

The footprints of the first people to walk on the Moon remain on its surface.

Apollo Program

Armstrong was part of the Apollo Program. Apollo 7 was the first of these missions to reach space. Apollo 8 was the first to reach the moon. But Apollo 11 was the first to land there. Apollo astronauts collected hundreds of pounds of samples for scientists to study on Earth.

The Saturn V rocket took the Apollo 11 astronauts to the Moon.

Astronauts and candidates to become astronauts for Artemis missions took a photo together in 2022.

Artemis Program

The last person on the Moon visited in 1972. NASA hoped to change that. The Artemis Program planned to land a crew on the Moon in 2025.

Dwarf planets can have moons.

What Makes a Planet?

A true planet must have three traits. First, it must orbit the Sun. Second, it must be round. Third, its gravity must be strong enough to clear its orbit. This means that a true planet's orbit doesn't have objects that are a similar size to that planet.

Dwarf Planets

A dwarf planet is a small planet. It is round like a planet. It orbits a star. But dwarf planets can't clear their orbits. They are too small. They do not have enough gravity.

Planet X

Another planet might be on the edge of the solar system. It could be as big as Neptune. Researchers call it Planet X.

Sedna might be a dwarf planet, but it is hard for scientists to tell because it is so far away.

The colors in this image of Pluto have been enhanced to show its surface textures.

Pluto

Pluto was once the ninth planet in the solar system. In 2006 that changed. Pluto was called a dwarf planet instead. It was the first dwarf planet identified in the solar system.

Pluto's Heart

In 2015 the *New Horizons* probe visited Pluto. It found that Pluto was one-third smaller than Earth's Moon. It took detailed photos of Pluto's surface. Pluto has many craters. But there is one smooth region that is shaped like a heart.

Pluto's Orbit

Pluto's orbit around the Sun is tilted compared with the planets' orbits.

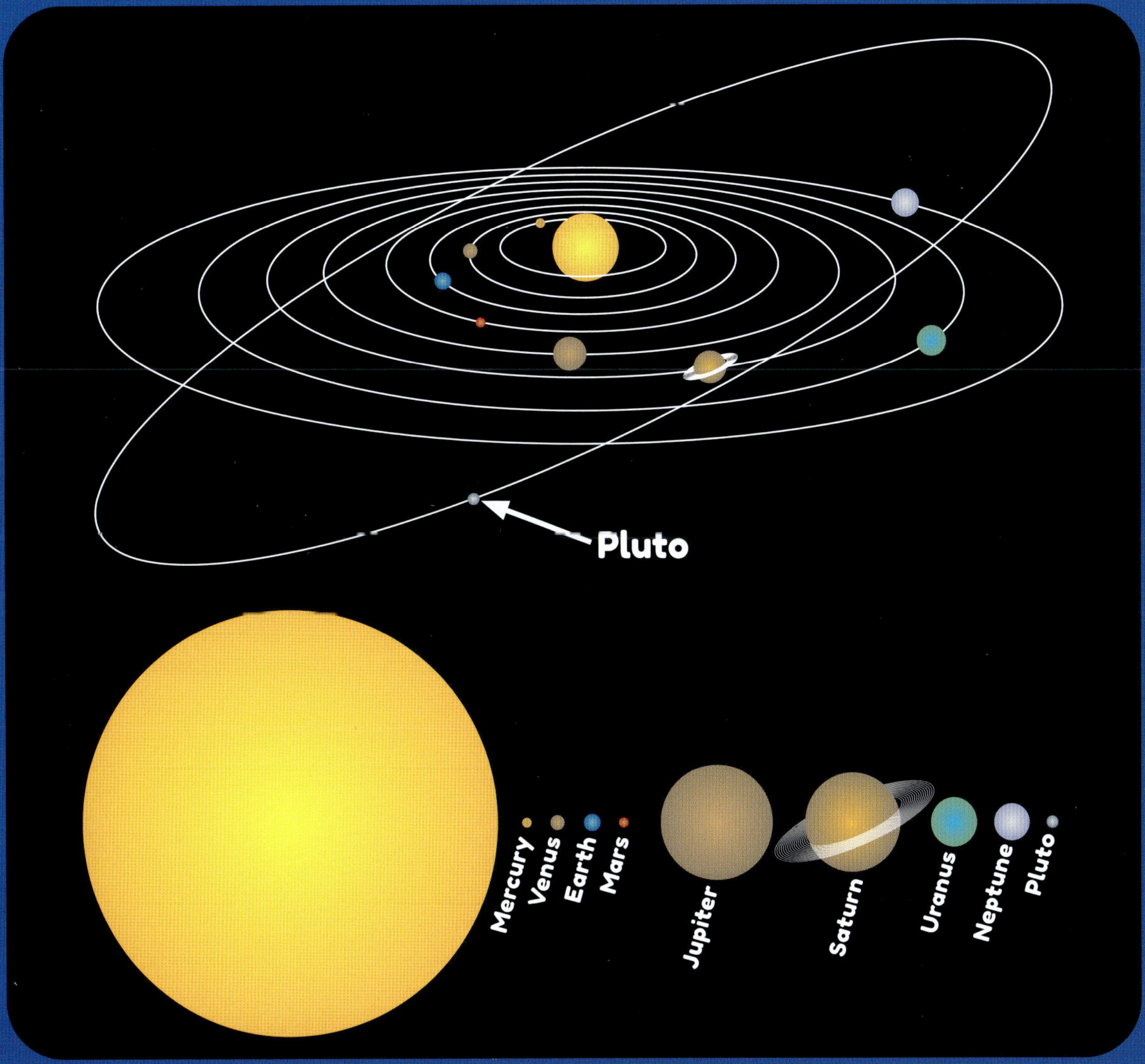

An illustration shows Makemake, which is named after a god of the Rapa Nui people of Easter Island.

Other Dwarf Planets

There are at least five dwarf planets in the solar system. These are Pluto, Ceres, Haumea, Makemake, and Eris. But more dwarf planets could be found.

Ceres

Ceres is located between Mars and Saturn. The dwarf planet is 13 times smaller than Earth. Its surface has some bright white spots. Researchers think this is salt.

FUN FACT!

The International Astronomical Union determines which objects are dwarf planets.

Ceres may have lots of water beneath its surface.

Haumea

If Earth were the size of a nickel, Haumea would be a sesame seed. This dwarf planet has rings. It also has two moons. It is shaped like an egg. That is because it spins quickly. One day lasts only four Earth hours.

An illustration shows Haumea, which is named after a Hawaiian goddess.

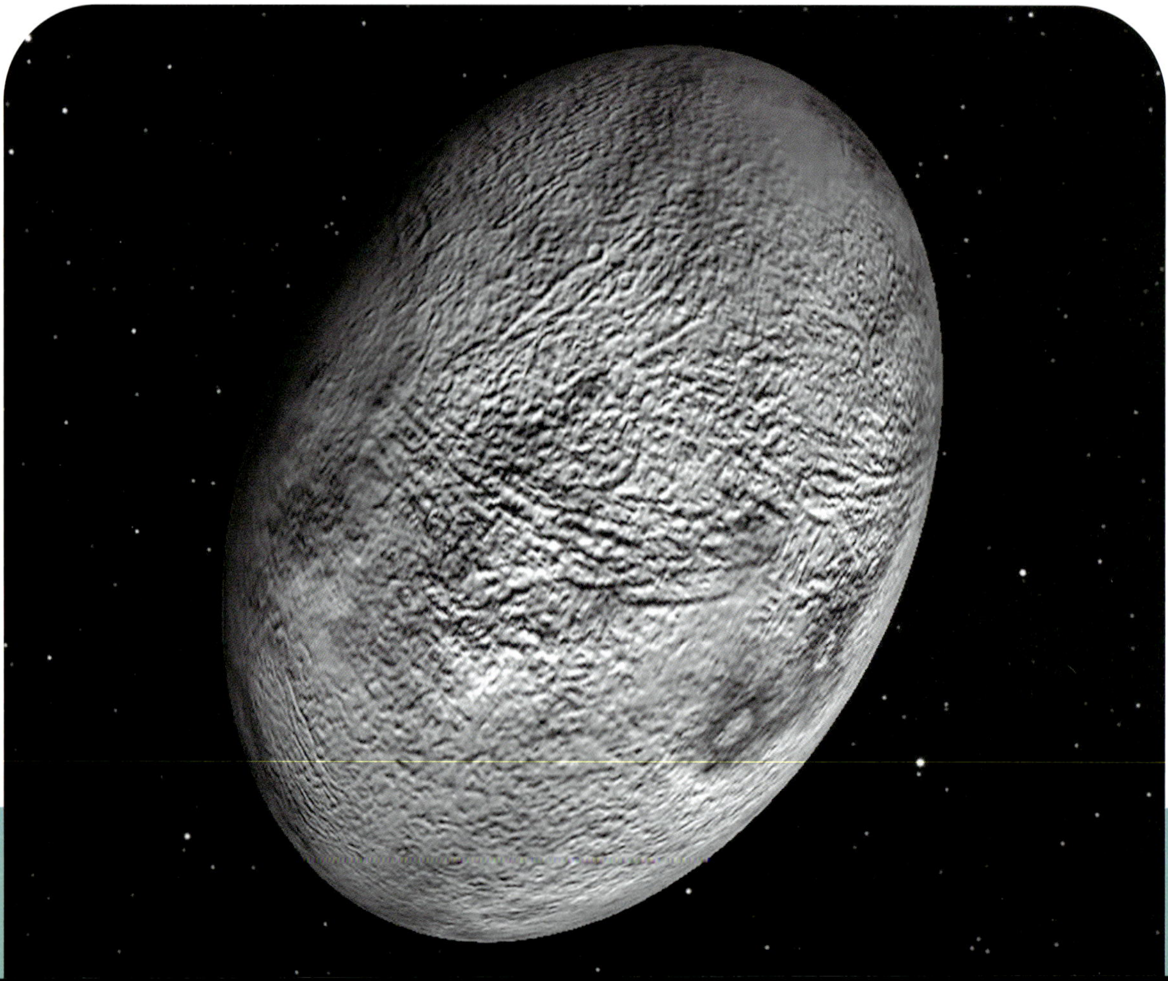

An illustration of Eris, which is about the same size as Pluto.

Eris

Eris is very far from the Sun. This dwarf planet is 6.2 billion miles (10 billion km) away from the Sun. That is 68 times farther than Earth. It takes 557 Earth years to orbit the Sun. It is so far that the atmosphere freezes. When it gets closer to the Sun, the atmosphere thaws.

The Perseid meteor shower occurs every year.

Rocks in Space

The Sun and planets make up almost all of the solar system's mass. But the solar system contains some other objects too. These include asteroids, comets, and meteoroids. Most are small. But some are hundreds of miles wide.

Clouds and Belts

Most of the rest of the remaining space objects are found in three places. Comets are found in the Oort Cloud and the Kuiper Belt. The Kuiper Belt is just outside Neptune's orbit. The Oort Cloud is at the far edge of the solar system. Asteroids are mostly in the asteroid belt. This belt is between Mars and Jupiter.

Kuiper Belt and Oort Cloud

The Kuiper Belt orbits the Sun.
The Oort Cloud surrounds the solar system.

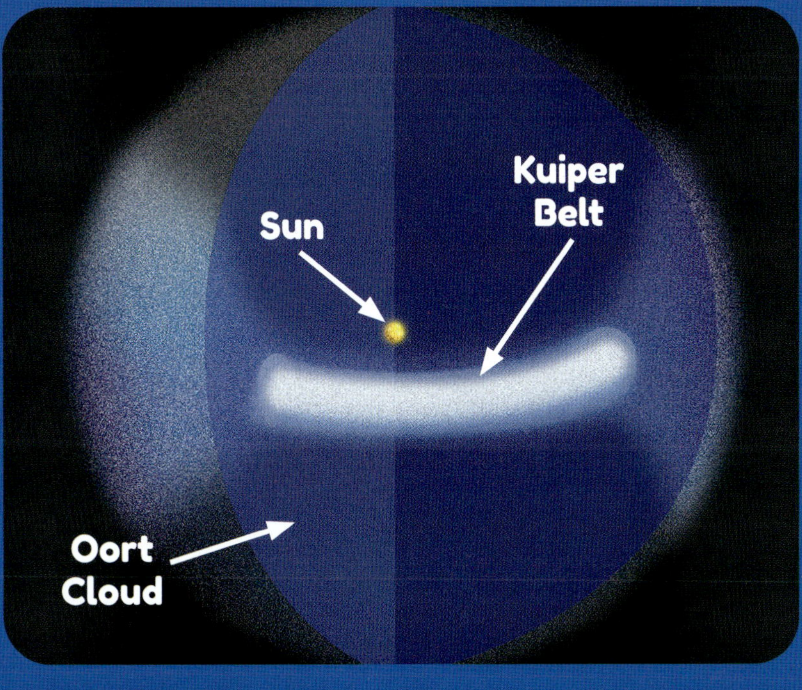

Asteroid Formation

Asteroids are rocky. NASA has counted more than 1 million asteroids in the solar system. They orbit the Sun. Most don't spin in one direction like planets do. Instead they tumble through space. They are made of clay, nickel, and iron.

Asteroid Names

There are few rules for naming asteroids. Some asteroids are named after famous singers. One is named after a pet cat.

Vesta is one of the largest asteroids in the asteroid belt.

An illustration shows NASA's *Double Asteroid Redirection Test* (*DART*) probe approaching Dimorphos.

Didymos

Didymos is an asteroid so large that another asteroid orbits it. Asteroids that orbit other asteroids are known as moonlets. Didymos's moonlet is called Dimorphos. Dimorphos was picked by NASA for a special test. NASA sent a probe to crash into it. The probe changed the moonlet's orbit. It was the first time a human-made object had changed the orbit of something in space.

Comets

Comets are icy. They orbit the Sun. Most of the time they are frozen. But when one gets near the Sun, it starts to melt. This causes dust and gas to blow into space. The dust and gas form a long tail behind the comet. The tail can be millions of miles long.

Halley's Comet

Halley's Comet is one of the solar system's most famous objects. It orbits the Sun every

In 2023 NASA had identified more than 3,900 comets.

The Bayeux Tapestry depicts a war between England and Normandy. It also shows Halley's Comet, *top center*.

76 Earth years. It flies close enough to Earth that humans can see it with the naked eye. The oldest recorded sighting was more than 2,000 years ago. It will next pass Earth in 2061.

Bayeux Tapestry

The Bayeux Tapestry is 230 feet (70 m) long. It was made in Europe in the 1000s CE. A comet is stitched in the tapestry. Historians think it is Halley's Comet.

When meteoroids enter Earth's atmosphere, they become meteorites. Big meteorites can leave craters, such as the Pingualuit Crater in Canada.

Meteoroids

Meteoroids are small rocks. Many are pieces of asteroids that have hit each other. Others have fallen off comets. There are a few that were once pieces of rocky planets.

Collisions

Meteoroids can travel up to 26 miles (42 km) per second. Even though they are small, they can create a lot of damage. Even a pebble-sized meteoroid could crack a spacecraft's window.

This piece of a meteorite hit Earth in 2018.

Star Formation

Stars are formed from large clouds of gas and dust. Gravity pulls the gas and dust together. They become dense. The pressure and temperature rise. A star is born once the temperature reaches 18 million degrees Fahrenheit (10 million°C).

Ordering Stars

Stars come in different shapes and sizes. Scientists divide stars into different groups. The groups are based on how bright and how hot the stars are.

Star Categories

Stars are grouped by size and temperature. Blue stars are the hottest, and red stars are the coolest.

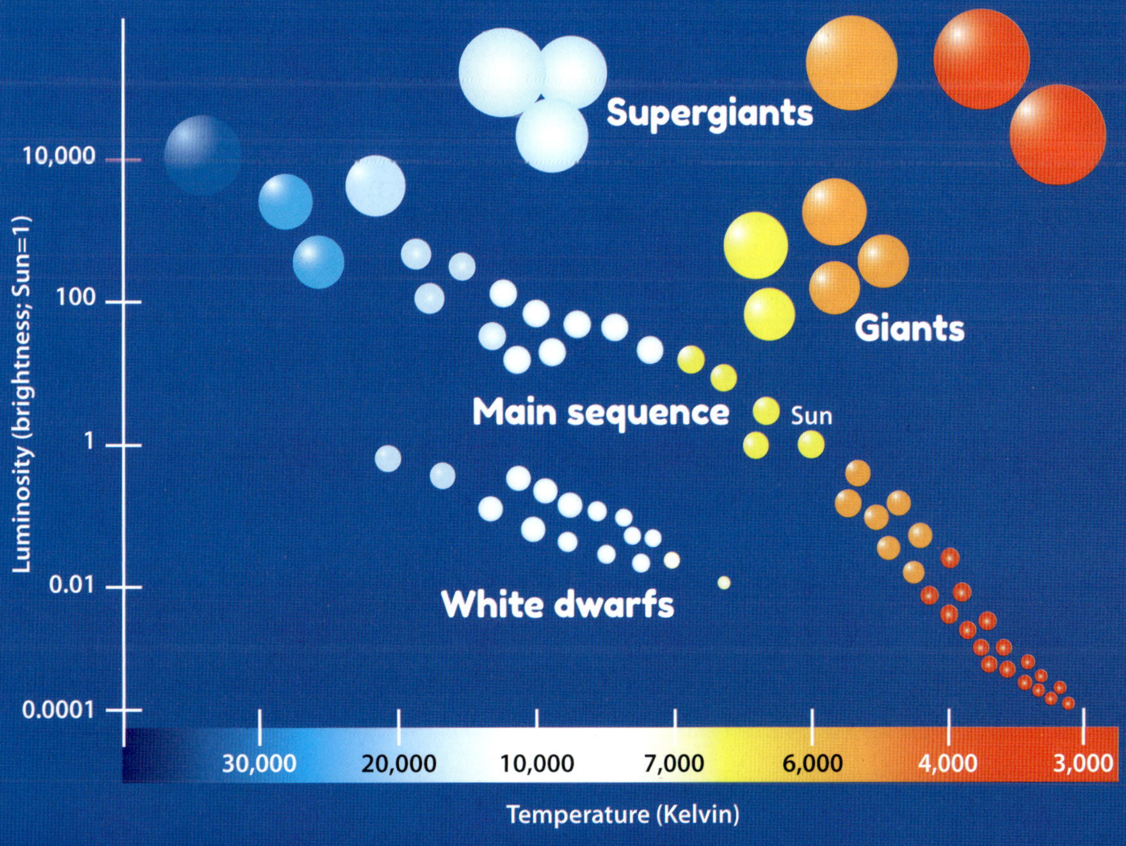

Main Sequence Stars

Most stars are grouped into the main sequence. The Sun is a main sequence star. About 90 percent of all stars are main sequence stars. They range from one-tenth to 200 times the Sun's mass.

Vega is a main sequence star.

Running Out of Fuel

Main sequence stars burn hydrogen as fuel. Eventually, that fuel runs out. The star's size determines what happens next.

About 97 percent of stars in the Milky Way will become white dwarfs.

Small Stars

Stars about the size of the Sun expand when they run out of fuel. They become red giants. The stars eventually cool and shrink. They end their lives as white dwarfs. On average, a white dwarf is only about the size of Earth.

Large Stars

Bigger stars become red supergiants when they run out of fuel. These huge stars eventually explode in a blast called a supernova. The hot gas left behind can be seen through telescopes from Earth.

FUN FACT!

Stars are born in gas clouds called stellar nurseries.

A star near the end of its life can have explosions that are similar to a supernova but do not destroy the star.

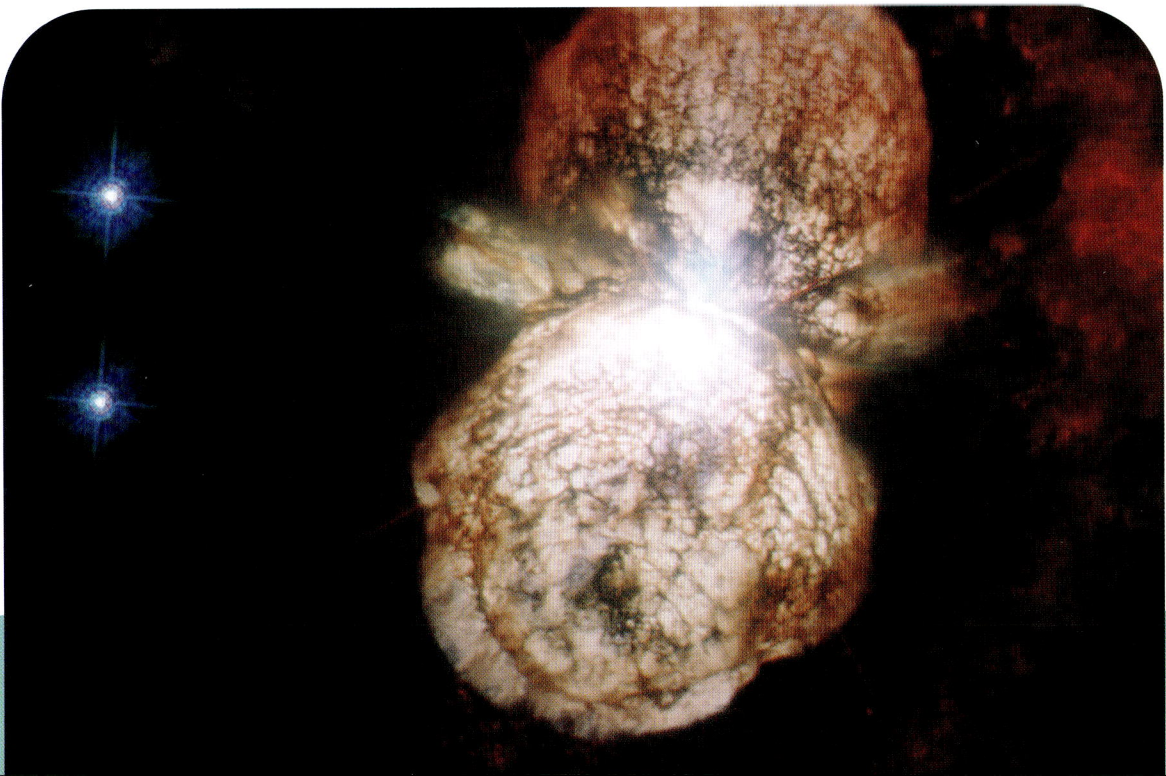

Neutron Stars and Black Holes

A supernova can form either a neutron star or a black hole. Neutron stars result from smaller stars. They are small and dense. Black holes result from larger stars. They are bodies in space with very high gravity. Not even light can escape their strong gravity. This makes them invisible.

An illustration shows what a black hole may look like in the middle of a galaxy.

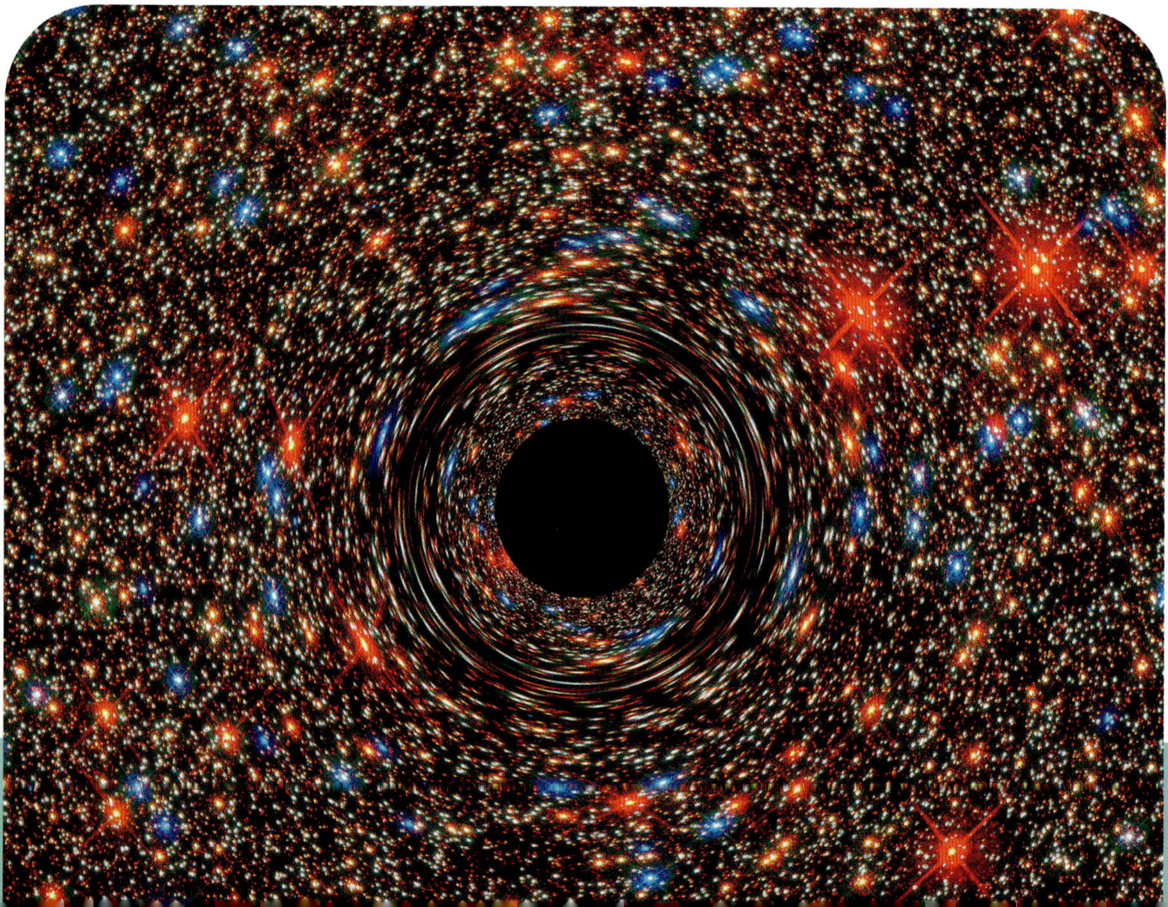

Binary stars can be close together.

Binary Star

Binary means "two." A binary star system has two stars. The stars orbit the same point in space. Many stars in the sky look like one point of light. However, more than 80 percent of them are actually binary systems.

GLOSSARY

active
When referring to volcanoes, a volcano that still erupts.

atmosphere
The gases that surround an object in space.

axis
An imaginary line through the center of a planet around which the planet spins.

crust
The upper solid layer of a planet.

dense
Tightly packed together.

evaporate
To turn from a liquid into a vapor.

galaxy
A group of stars and other space objects that are kept near each other by gravity.

horizon
The line where the surface of a large body in space visually meets the sky.

horizontally
Side to side.

magma
Hot, melted rock inside a planet or other body.

orbiter
A spacecraft that orbits an object in space.

particle
A small piece of matter.

probe
A spacecraft that gathers information and sends it back to Earth.

satellite
A spacecraft that orbits an object in space, usually Earth.

vertically
Up and down.

TO LEARN MORE

More Books to Read

Dendy, Christina. *Physical Science*. Abdo, 2025.

Gater, Will. *The Mysteries of the Universe*. DK, 2020.

Murray, Julie. *Rovers*. Abdo, 2020.

Online Resources

Booklinks
NONFICTION NETWORK
FREE! ONLINE NONFICTION RESOURCES

To learn more about space, please visit **abdobooklinks.com** or scan this QR code. These links are routinely monitored and updated to provide the most current information available.

INDEX

PHOTO CREDITS

Cover Photos: Marko Aliaksandr/Shutterstock Images, front (comet); Dima Zel/Shutterstock Images, front (Earth); Shutterstock Images, front (galaxy); Alex Konon/Shutterstock Images, front (night); Lukasz Pawel Szczepanski/Shutterstock Images, front (Sun); M. Aurelius/Shutterstock Images, back

Interior Photos: Vadim Sadovski/Shutterstock Images, 1, 21; Aleksandr Lysenko/Shutterstock Images, 3; Jose M. Diego, Jordan C. J. D'Silva, Anton M. Koekemoer, Jake Summers, Rogier Windhorst, and Haojing Yan/STScI/CSA/ESA/NASA, 4; Shutterstock Images, 5, 8, 9, 37 (bottom), 39, 41, 96, 105, 119; NASA, 6, 10 (top), 11, 12, 15, 24, 26, 27, 28, 30, 31, 34, 35, 36, 42, 44, 45, 47, 49, 50, 52, 53, 58, 61, 62, 66 (top), 68, 72, 74, 76, 80, 82–83, 87, 88, 89, 90, 91, 92, 94, 97, 99, 100, 103 (bottom), 107, 112 (bottom); Lars Poyansky/Shutterstock Images, 7; Akito Studio/Shutterstock Images, 10 (bottom), 33 (bottom), 37 (top), 48 (bottom), 63 (top), 66 (bottom), 81 (bottom), 103 (top); Leif Heimbold/NASA, 13; Carnegie Institution of Washington/Johns Hopkins University Applied Physics Laboratory/NASA, 14, 17, 18, 19, 20, 23; Genna Duberstein/Goddard Space Flight Center/NASA, 16; National Air and Space Museum, 22; Terrance Emerson/Shutterstock Images, 25; Richard Bizley/Science Source, 29; Akihiko Ikeshita/JAXA/JIJI Press/AFP/Getty Images, 32; J. Greaves/Cardiff University/JAXA/AP Images, 33 (top); Dominic Jeanmaire/Shutterstock Images, 38; Andrew Mayovskyy/Shutterstock Images, 40; Bill Anders/NASA, 43; University of Arizona/JPL-Caltech/NASA, 46; Texas A&M University/University of Arizona/JPL-Caltech/NASA, 48 (top); Arizona State University/JPL/NASA, 51; A. Simon/ESA/NASA, 54; Christopher Go/NASA, 55; Alan Dyer/Stocktrek Images/Science Source, 56; Space Science Institute/JPL/NASA, 57, 64, 69, 70; University of Arizona/JPL/NASA, 59, 60; ESA/ATG medialab/NASA/J. Nichols/JPL/University of Arizona/DLR/Science Source, 63 (bottom); Space Science Institute/JPL-Caltech/NASA, 65, 71; Mark Garlick/Science Photo Library/Getty Images, 67; Steve Gribben/Johns Hopkins Applied Physics Laboratory/NASA, 73, 113; Wikimedia Commons, 75, 85, 95, 115 (top); Lawrence Sromovsky/W. W. Keck Observatory/NASA, 77; Kevin M. Gill/JPL-Caltech/NASA, 78; Diego Barucco/Shutterstock Images, 79; John R. Foster/Science Source, 81 (top); Mark Garlick/Science Source, 83; Justin Cowart/Voyager-ISS/JPL/NASA, 84; SkyPics Studio/Shutterstock Images, 86; Universities Space Research Association/Lunar & Planetary Institute/JPL/NASA, 93; Lunar Reconnaissance Orbi/NASA, 98; Kim Shiflett/NASA, 101; Ron Miller/Science Source, 102; Southwest Research Institute/Johns Hopkins University Applied Physics Laboratory/NASA, 104; Jin Zan/Wikimedia Commons, 106, 108; L. Calçada and Nick Risinger/ESO, 109; Bill Ingalls/NASA/Getty Images News/Getty Images, 110; Tim Brown/Science Source, 111; Ninja Studio/Shutterstock Images, 112 (top), 115 (bottom); Hulton Archive/Getty Images, 114; Japan ASTER Science Team/Japan Space Systems and US/AIST/METI/NASA, 116; Steve Jurvetson/Flickr, 117; Dmitry Sedakov/Shutterstock Images, 118; John Colosimo/ESO, 120; Scott Wiessinger/Goddard Space Flight Center/NASA, 121; Z. Levay/ESA/NASA, 122; A. Goobar and the Hubble Heritage Team/ESA/NASA, 123; D. Coe, J. Anderson, and R. van der Marel/ESA/NASA, 124; L. Calçada/ESO, 125